SADDLED UP

PENNY BIRCH

Published by Xcite Books Ltd – 2011

Print ISBN 9781907761843

Printed and bound in the UK

Cover design by
Adam Walker

Chapter One

Some girls need to be spanked.

I need to be spanked anyway, not often, but just occasionally. It's not because I'm naughty and deserve to be punished, although sometimes I wish it was, but because it fulfils a deep need in me. All my life I've fought against that need, but never managed to conquer it. Far more often I'm the one doing the spanking, but when I do need my own bottom dealt with, I need it too badly to hold back, and I need it done properly.

Which is why I was driving down a narrow lane just off the A1 with my heart in my mouth and my bottom packed into a pair of ridiculous little jeans shorts that left most of my cheeks spilling out at the sides. That's the trouble with being the sort of girl who needs to be spanked. You have to find somebody to do the spanking. That's not easy for me. I find it hard to submit, and really hard to submit to men. So it has to be a woman, and it has to be a woman big enough and strong enough to hold me in place. That's where Hannah Riley comes in. She's built like a dray horse and she knows exactly how to handle me, over her knee and my panties pulled down without any nonsense for a good, old-fashioned, bare-bottom spanking.

I like it that way, nothing fancy, just the classic routine; my zip unfastened to make it easier for her to take my shorts down, over her knee with my hips lifted so that she can get me bare, shorts pulled down to show off my panties, panties

1

pulled down to show off my bare bottom and her massive hand applied to my cheeks as she spanks me. It leaves me hot and shaking, dizzy with reaction and helpless to resist, in a state of ecstasy that comes no other way. Naturally there's a price, which is to please her in turn, and sometimes other people, because I have to accept her rules or I won't get it at all.

That's why I was in the silly little jeans shorts, which I wouldn't normally wear, ever. She likes me in shorts, with plenty of cheek showing, and not just for the view I provide. I find it humiliating and she knows it, while she also feels that having to show off my bottom keeps me in my place. It certainly keeps me conscious of my rear view, and I try very hard to make sure nobody else sees. She likes people to see, especially men, which is a bit of a problem. Men have never been easy for me, but once I've been spanked, and with Hannah in charge, I really can't help myself.

Hannah's a traveller, of sorts, and while the site where she'd told me I'd find her caravan was convenient it was also rather too close to my house for comfort, just a few miles across country. Yet I hadn't seen anybody at all on the lane and the tension in my belly faded a little as the satnav told me I'd reached my destination and I realised that I probably wasn't going to have to show off my bottom after all, at least not to anybody other than the woman I'd asked to spank it. With my relief came a stab of disappointment, in turn leaving me feeling ever so slightly ashamed of myself for my dirty thoughts as I drove slowly on, expecting to find her caravan parked alongside the track.

Eventually the hedge to my left gave way to an open area of broken tarmac and flat slabs of concrete that must once have been the bases of huts but now supported not one caravan, but two, also several cars and an open truck filled with old white goods and scrap metal. A large, dun-coloured billy-goat was tethered nearby, the only sign of life, and for a moment my feelings of tension began to wane, only to grow stronger once more as two men stepped out from behind the truck. Both were typically Irish, one tall and strongly built with a mop of thick black hair and a handsome but somehow mocking face, the other taller still but cane-thin, lanky and extraordinarily ugly, with straggling red hair, buck teeth and a little pointed beard that looked as if the moths had been at it. Their clothes were scruffy to say the least, but I was hardly in a position to criticise with half my bottom sticking out of my shorts, and the thought of them seeing set me warm and pink with embarrassment.

I parked as close as I could to Hannah's caravan and got out, trying to ignore the curious glances of the two men. There was so much debris around that I had a good ten yards to go, and no chance of concealing the way I was dressed. One of them whistled and my face grew hotter still as I hurried to the door. I could feel their eyes on me as I knocked, their gaze lingering on the swell of my bottom and shape of my cheeks where they bulged from my shorts. Both were vaguely familiar from previous expeditions, and I found myself wondering just how much they knew, bringing my blushes up to red heat as I imagined them laughing together over my spanking, perhaps even peering in at a window to watch me get it, bare bottom over Hannah's lap with my cheeks bouncing to the slaps and the lips of my fanny showing between my thighs. I very nearly ran back to my car, but then the door had swung open to reveal a heavy-set woman in a pink bathrobe held half-closed over a nightie, not Hannah, but her friend Maggie.

'Oh, it's you, Amber,' she said, her voice thick with contempt. 'Hannah, your tart's here.'

She hadn't even bothered to keep her voice down, and I heard laughter from the men behind me as I hurried into the caravan. Maggie was smoking, as always, and the place was thick with the smell of cigarettes and cheap perfume, making me retch as I pushed the door closed. My hand was shaking so badly I fumbled the handle, while the heat in my

3

face and neck was making my skin prickle, so strong was my embarrassment, for the men outside, and for Maggie, because her presence didn't mean I'd be let off my spanking, only that I'd have an audience. Quite possibly they'd take turns with me.

Hannah appeared from behind a curtain at the far end of the caravan, her imposing bulk putting Maggie to shame. She was also in her night things, a huge, pale green baby-doll with a fluffy trim, the semi-transparent material clinging to her colossal breasts and swollen stomach. As always, just to look at her made me feel weak, and set me wondering how I could possibly want to be punished by her even as I was filled with an overwhelming desire for exactly that. I had to be insane to let her do what she did to me, and yet my fingers had already gone to the button of my shorts, ready to make myself vulnerable, or push them straight down if she told me to.

'Hold yer horses, love,' she growled. 'I ain't even had a cup of tea yet.'

I nodded weakly in response as she stumped over to the chair in which she liked to sit while she spanked me, flopping down with a grunt. Maggie had already gone to the tiny galley, where she busied herself with the tea-making preparation I'd evidently interrupted. I stayed as I was, feeling more embarrassed than ever, until Hannah spoke again.

'You can take 'em off if you want. We don't care.'

'No, thank you …' I began, and trailed off, unable to explain that I liked to have my shorts pulled down by her, or at the very least be ordered out of them.

'Suit yourself,' she said. 'It's all the same in the end.'

'Thinks she's too good for us, that's her problem,' Maggie remarked, which was completely unfair when we all three knew that I was soon going to be bare bottom across Hannah's lap, and had been many times before.

'Not at all,' I said, then stopped once more, painfully

4

aware that any attempt to explain my true feelings was only going to make matters worse.

After all, I did think I was too good for them, at least in the sense that they were very definitely of the people and I wasn't, which was what she meant. That was one of the things which really brought out my feelings when Hannah spanked me, knowing that I was being firmly put in my place by a coarse, working-class woman. It was just so inappropriate, so utterly demeaning, the perfect humiliation. I'd never had the courage to tell her and didn't intend to start now, for all that I was sure she got a lot of extra pleasure out of our encounters precisely because of my wealthy background.

Maggie passed a mug of tea to Hannah and took up a second for herself, leaving me to collect mine. As I passed her she slapped my bottom, to set me blushing again and making the trembling of my hands so bad I could barely hold my tea without spilling it. She sat down, leaving me standing in front of them, fidgeting with my mug and blowing on my tea to try and cool it down a little. Hannah took a sip from her own mug, blew out her breath and then looked up at me.

'So you met Leary and Sean?'

'The men outside? I saw them, yes.'

She gave a dirty chuckle that sent a powerful shiver right through me at the thought of the possibilities offered by the presence of the two men. It wasn't beyond her to invite them in to watch me being spanked, or worse, making me strip for them, even suck their cocks. I really didn't want to do it, but I knew I would if she told me to, filling me with fresh shame but at the same time setting my so nipples stiff they were making sizeable bumps through my bra and top. Maggie noticed and laughed.

'Eager are we? Come on then, how about we have those fat tits out?'

'Yes, get them out,' Hannah ordered.

Hannah usually pulled my top clothes up when she spanked me anyway, both to humiliate me and because she liked to touch my breasts, so I didn't protest, putting down my tea and lifting my top and bra to let them spill free.

'Hold them up,' she ordered. 'Play with your nips.'

I obeyed, cupping my breasts and running my fingers over my stiff nipples. Both little buds of flesh felt sensitive and I couldn't hold back a sigh of pleasure. Maggie gave a derisive snort for my obvious arousal.

'Tart.'

'Get your top off,' Hannah ordered, 'and your bra. I like my girls topless.'

Again I obeyed, peeling off before I went back to my tea, now completely naked from the waist up. I'd been made to go like that before, and nude, generally after my spanking, flaunting my red bottom as I tidied up her caravan for her or cooked her a meal in nothing but a pinny. It amused her to see me naked, or better still half-naked but made ridiculous in some way, so her next order came as no surprise.

'Pull your shorts up tight, right up between those big cheeks. Let's see it all.'

I hesitated, telling myself that as I was going to be spanked anyway a refusal would make little difference. An instant and I'd thought better of it, catching hold of the waistband of my shorts and wriggling them tight up into my bottom slit to leave both cheeks fully exposed the way she wanted. Showing defiance was all very well, but it was more than likely to earn me the hairbrush, and not only the flat across my bottom cheeks but quite possibly the handle stuck up the tight little hole between them.

Most of my bum was now out of my shorts, a display as rude as it was silly, and as I went back to my tea I was acutely conscious of the state I was in, my breasts bare, my bottom spilling out of my jeans shorts and the material at the front pulled up so tight against my fanny that every detail of my lips showed. Twice Maggie had called me a tart and I

6

could see her point. I certainly looked like one. Now she laughed.

'I can see your panties.'

It was true, the white cotton sticking out around the hem of my shorts where I'd pulled them up tight, adding one more ridiculous detail to the way I looked. Hannah also chuckled to see the state I was in, then adjusted herself in her chair, moving forward just far enough to make a lap. My stomach went tight at the implication, because I'd thought I had a few minutes more of being made to show myself off while she finished her tea, but there was no mistaking the meaning of her gesture as she patted one tree-trunk thigh, or her words.

'Come on then, let's give you what you need.'

I got down, unfastening the button on my jeans shorts even as I bent to place myself across her lap and into that wonderful, awful pose, over another woman's knee with my bottom lifted for spanking. She put one heavy arm around my waist, trapping me in position, and took a grip on my shorts to pull them tighter still into the slit of my bottom. A sharp tug and I was gasping as I was lifted by my shorts, leaving me with my cheeks on yet more blatant show and only a strip of denim and my dishevelled panties to hide the details of my anus and fanny. My bottom felt huge, plump and pink behind me, a great wobbling ball of girl flesh so big and round that I deserved spanking just for being built that way.

Hannah began to touch me up, caressing my cheeks and teasing in my slit, making no effort whatsoever to hide her enjoyment of my body. It was always that way, the actual spanking more my need than hers, but that wasn't going to stop her doing it, or spare me any pain. Sure enough, she'd soon started to smack, gently at first, just to make my bottom bounce and watch the way my flesh moved to the slaps, then harder, full across my sweet spot until I'd began to gasp and kick my legs.

7

I couldn't see Maggie, but I knew she was watching, enjoying the view of my bouncing bottom. Like Hannah she got off on the sight of me bare as much as the spanking, but she had one or two nasty little habits of her own. Not that it mattered, because my bottom was already beginning to warm and I knew that once I'd been properly spanked I'd be unable to resist, whatever they might want to do with me.

'Time we had these down,' Hannah grunted and the spanking had paused while her hand went to the waistband of my shorts.

My hips came up to make it easier for her, and as she began to tug them down I closed my eyes, lost in the shame of having my bottom exposed. Not that I'd been hiding much, but the feel of my shorts being jerked roughly down over my cheeks was still so strong that it brought me to the edge of tears. I was being stripped, my boobs already out and my panties no doubt to follow in short order.

They were still in my slit, protecting nothing as Hannah went back to spanking me, save those two all-important details, my bottom hole and my fanny. I could feel the material, sticky and wet on my sex where I'd started to juice, but they were still a barrier, a barrier I needed removed. Maggie laughed to see me so wet and so eager, and because I was sticking my bottom up to Hannah's slaps in the hope of having my panties pulled down.

'You can see what she wants!' she said. 'Go on, let's have that fat little cunt showing.'

Her words brought a sob to my throat and then it was being done, my panties tugged out of my bottom slit and pulled down around my thighs. That was it, two quick jerks and I was bare behind, my fanny and bumhole on show as the spanking began once more. It was harder now, powerful smacks full across the crest of my cheeks, and fast, so much so that I'd quickly lost control, bucking up and down on Hannah's lap and kicking my thighs in my shorts and panties. She clung on, keeping me firmly in place as she

8

spanked me, then abruptly hooking one foot around my leg, to hold me more securely still and incidentally spreading my bottom cheeks wide open.

Now they could really see everything, my wet, open fanny, puffy with excitement, the brownish ring and bright pink centre of my bumhole, winking in my pain and helpless exasperation for what was being done to me. Maggie laughed again, louder than before, encouraging Hannah to spread me wider still and to spank even harder. With that I lost control completely and burst into tears, sobbing my heart out across her lap as my bottom and boobies bounced to the furious rhythm of my spanking.

'Cry baby,' Maggie remarked.

'She always was,' Hannah agreed.

'Soft as shit, these posh girls, and they're all the same.'

Hannah merely grunted and began to spank harder still, until I was writhing in her grip, my hair tossing and my legs pumping, lost to all sense of decency. As usual she'd reduced me to a squalling, spanked brat within a few minutes of my arrival, and it wasn't going to be long before she'd reduced me further still. My bottom was on fire, the juice running freely from my open fanny, my hole wide and ready for penetration. If she'd invited the men from outside to take turns with me I'd have been on my knees with one cock in my mouth and another in my hand in seconds, then happily sticking my bottom up for rear entry while they took turns with me and I licked cunt for the women.

That wasn't the deal, not today, but I knew they'd be able to hear my squeals and the sound of Hannah's palm against my flesh, and that there could be only one possible interpretation of those noises, that the girl they'd seen go into the caravan was now being spanked. The thought drew fresh tears from my eyes, and when the spanking suddenly stopped I was left blubbering across Hannah's lap with my bottom stuck high and wide, my twins holes an open invitation for entry.

I got it, a finger up my cunt then wiped on my hot bottom flesh before Hannah set to work once more, only this time with her hairbrush. Maggie gave a crow of laughter and slapped her leg in delight at my squeal of shock and pain. I hadn't even known Hannah had the hairbrush ready, but now realised that she must have put it aside specially in order to give me a surprise. She'd succeeded, because it hurt far more than her hand, so that she had me kicking and writhing again on the instant, so hard that one of my shoes came off. There was a crash, Maggie swore and my spanking stopped abruptly.

'You stupid little cow!' Hannah spat. 'Can't you be more careful?'

She'd loosened her grip and I craned around, to find that my shoe had knocked over my half finished mug of tea, spilling it on the patterned linoleum that covered the caravan floor. I found myself apologising immediately, for all that it wasn't my fault at all, but I got no sympathy.

'You can mop that up,' Hannah ordered, releasing me.

'With your knickers,' Maggie added.

I didn't even think to resist, slumping to the floor and peeling off my shorts and panties to leave me in nothing but short white socks and a single shoe. My bottom was on fire, my whole body shaking with reaction, my vision a blur of tears as I set to work, crawling on the floor to mop at the spilt tea with my panties. They watched in silence, save for Hannah's breathing, which had grown hoarse from the exertion of spanking me. Soon I'd finished and I turned to them, kneeling, my filthy, sodden panties clutched in one hand, my chest heaving. I was wet with sweat, my nipples stiff and my fanny moist and swollen, fully ready for what was coming and as Hannah began to pull up her nightie I was already crawling across the floor.

'Good girl,' she sighed. 'Now just you get busy for Auntie Hannah, eh?'

'You little tart,' Maggie added as I reached my place

10

between Hannah's thighs.

She had nothing on underneath, and as her thighs came open I was presented with her broad, red cunt, the slit damp with juice beneath a fat mound thickly grown with coarse black pubes. I hesitated and she immediately caught me by my hair, dragging me in to press my face to her wet, musky flesh. My mouth came wide and I'd began to lick at her outsize clitoris, eager to please and disgusted with myself all at the same time, but not so disgusted that my fingers hadn't quickly slipped between my thighs.

I was soaking, and so sensitive that I knew I'd come in just moments. My other hand went back too and I'd begun to stroke my bottom, feeling my hot flesh as I rubbed at my eager cunt and pleasured the woman who'd given me my spanking. I felt the first contractions as my orgasm started to build, only to have Hannah reach forward and pull my arms roughly towards her.

'Oh no you don't, you greedy little bitch,' she growled. 'I get it first.'

Her grip was far too strong for me to break, as I knew from bitter experience of past spankings, so I didn't even try to struggle but gave my full attention to her sex. She didn't let go, holding my arms right up, painfully hard, with my hands on her breasts. I began to knead her flesh and rub my thumbs over her nipples, in pain but in ecstasy too, just for the way she was handling me. Maggie had leant forward, and laughed as she began to spank me once more, using Hannah's hairbrush to encourage me to lick harder.

I was already doing the best I could, but the smacks on my already burning bottom drove me higher still, until I was gasping and sobbing out my passion into Hannah's cunt. She came, unexpectedly, crushing my head between her thighs until I couldn't breath and holding me in place as shudder after shudder ran through her. When she finally let go I was gasping for breath, my tongue sore and my face sticky with her juices. Again I tried to get my fingers to my sex, but

11

Maggie had hold of me immediately.

She was on the edge of her chair, fat thighs spread wide and pink nylon knickers held to one side to show off her cunt. I was dragged in, my face buried in wet, hairy flesh and for the second time I began to lick. Like Hannah, she was hurting me, her hand twisted in my hair, but again it brought me more pleasure than pain and my fingers were soon busy between my legs. This time I was determined to make it, and unlike Hannah, Maggie didn't seem to care. As my contractions began once more I let my mind focus, on the way they'd humiliated me and made me strip, how Hannah had spanked my bare bottom and made me mop up spilt tea with my own panties, how much it hurt as they made me lick cunt, but best of all how for all that they'd done to me I was now kneeling in the nude with my fingers busy in my wet, squashy cunt as I masturbated shamelessly in front of them.

I came, riding my orgasm as I licked at Maggie's sex, completely lost in the ecstasy of my own abuse, one dizzying peak and then a second, followed by a final shiver of pleasure at the sound of Hannah's laughter for the disgraceful exhibition I was making of myself. With that it was over. Maggie had come as I did, a short, hard orgasm I barely noticed but for a grunt and a twist of her hand in my hair. I was still coming down as she let go and I kept my face buried in her sex for a moment more before pulling away with two heartfelt words.

'Thank you.'

'Any time, ducks,' Hannah replied. 'Make her another cuppa, Maggie. She looks like she needs one.'

I did, but as I cleaned up and dressed I was in a state of pure bliss, so happy with myself I couldn't stop smiling or resist the temptation to admire my rear view in the mirror. My bottom was very red, with bruises in a couple of places where the hairbrush had caught me, and even with my shorts pulled up it was very obvious that I'd been spanked. I knew

I'd stay that way for quite a while, so would have to dash to the car or risk giving Sean and Leary a show. Not that they could have failed to notice, with the noise I'd made while Hannah was dealing with me, a thought that left me blushing again, but smiling too.

'Do they know, Leary and Sean?' I asked.

'They do now,' Maggie chuckled.

'Not the truth of it,' Hannah put in, 'only that I believe in spanking.'

I nodded and accepted a mug of tea from Maggie. It was hot and sweet, and my feelings gradually settled down as I drank. My punishment had been exactly what I needed, hard enough to hurt but not too extreme and sufficiently humiliating to allow me to let go completely. I knew what was coming too, euphoria, then a drop, after which it would be a few weeks until I needed it again, all in time with my natural cycle.

We talked of this and that as I drank my tea, after which I made my excuses. The only thing we really had in common was my need to be punished and the pleasure Hannah took in dishing it out, so our conversation was always a bit awkward, and all the more so for Maggie's resentment of my background, which she didn't seem to be able to get over. I thanked them again as I stood to leave, poking my head out of the caravan door in the hope of a clear run to my car without having to show my smacked bottom off to Leary and Sean.

It was hopeless. They were not only still there but obviously waiting for me, both loitering by the truck even though it was now unloaded. Yet I could just do it, if I walked round the front of my car instead of the back, a seemingly odd thing to do but better than giving them a show of my smacked bottom. I set off, walking fast with the colour rising in my cheeks as I drew closer. As I reached the shelter of the car I caught the clip-clop of hooves and turned my head to see two riders approaching down the lane, both young women in smart hacking jackets, one dark, one with startling red hair and thick rimmed glasses.

They were talking together and hadn't seen me, but they were going to at any second and it couldn't have been worse. There was no mistaking the implication of my red cheeks, and I'd rather have shown off my smacked bottom to a dozen leering travellers, gone nude for a hundred dirty old men to masturbate over my rosy cheeks, been spanked naked in front of a thousand selected perverts, anything but have two cool, aloof young ladies see what had been done to me. Maggie's amusement and contempt I could cope with, but not theirs, and to make matters worse they were just the sort of people who were likely to come into my shop.

I darted for the door of my car, snatching the handle even as I thrust my hand into the pocket of my jeans shorts, to find it empty. My keys were gone, and they weren't in the other pocket either, which meant they had to have fallen out when I stripped. For one awful moment I just stood there like an idiot, jumping up and down on my feet with my red bottom jiggling behind me as I frantically searched my pockets, but really there was only one thing for it, a dash for the caravan. That meant Leary and Sean would see everything, maybe the girls as well, but if I didn't run they were going to see anyway. I ran.

The cheeks of my face can't have been any less red than those of my bum as I sprinted for the caravan door. One of the men made a remark I didn't catch and the other laughed, but it wasn't them I was worried about, not any more. As I grabbed the door handle it seemed to stick, giving me a horrid vision of myself standing there waiting for Hannah or Maggie to open it while the girls rode slowly past with a prime view of my bottom in the ridiculous little shorts with my reddened cheeks sticking out around the side. At last it came open and I tumbled inside, gasping out my explanation to the two astonished woman even as Hannah held out my keys to me.

14

'Something the matter?'

She knew, because she was having trouble keeping the smile from her face, while Maggie was smirking openly. I thanked her as I retrieved my keys, but I was wondering if she'd taken them on purpose, also whether she'd seen the two girls. Not that I really cared, too grateful for the shelter of the caravan to worry about anything else.

A peep through the curtains allowed me to check that the coast was clear before I once more set off for my car, full of chagrin and not even bothering to go around the front to spare myself the attention of Leary and Sean. After all, they'd already seen. They also knew I was in a state, but that didn't stop the handsome one from making a remark as I passed, although there was a hint of sympathy in his voice.

'Got it from Fat Hannah, did you?'

I found my mouth twitching up into an embarrassed smile despite everything, but there was a lump in my throat that felt as if I'd swallowed an egg whole and I could find no words. Not that there was any point in trying to deny what had happened and I found myself nodding weakly as I moved on to my car.

'She's a bad one for walloping girls' arses, is Fat Hannah,' the skinny one said, and he also sounded sympathetic.

Suddenly the tears were starting from my eyes again and I hurriedly climbed into the car so that they wouldn't see. It was just too much for me, my emotions too raw to handle, not so much for what had been done to me, nor even for the embarrassing episode with the keys, but because Leary and Sean thought I'd been spanked to punish me. They didn't know I liked it. They didn't know about my arrangement with Hannah. All they knew was that I'd gone into Hannah's caravan, and that for some reason she'd found it necessary to spank me.

It was unbearably shameful, and unbearably exciting. They would soon realise that I was crying too, and I had to

15

get away before they came to talk to me. Explaining was out of the question, which meant letting them comfort me as if I was a naughty girl who'd had to be spanked, no doubt all the while with their cocks hard for the thought of what had been done to me and how I'd have looked over Hannah's knee. I had to get away, fast.

I started the car, blinking tears from my eyes as I swung away from the caravans, but I was in no state to drive. Maybe I'd be all right on the lane, but not in traffic. I had to stop, just as soon as I was far enough away to be absolutely certain they wouldn't follow me. A quarter mile seemed enough and I pulled in at a farm gate to sit back in my seat, my eyes scrunched up and the tears streaming down my face as I struggled to control the thoughts racing through my head.

After a minute or so I'd calmed down enough to find some tissues and wipe my tears away, but I still didn't feel I'd be safe to drive. My breathing was ragged and deep, while I couldn't get what had happened out of my head. Each time I thought of Leary and Sean a little shudder passed through me, not for them, but because they knew I'd been spanked and they thought I'd been punished. I knew what I had to do, bring myself to orgasm again, and the instant I got home, or sooner.

There was nobody in the lane, which stretched straight and empty in front and behind. If anybody came past I would see them long before they could see me, let alone what I was doing, while the gate was old and rotten with grass and brambles, making it impossible to open. Nobody was going to come that way. All I needed to do was unbutton my shorts and slip a hand down the front. I'd be there in seconds.

Still I hesitated, but the only sounds were the distant throb of traffic on the main road and the occasional snatch of birdsong. Even if another car came past they wouldn't see, and any walker would have to be right next to my window, and deliberately looking in, to realise what I was up to. It had to be safe, and I was going to do it. My shorts came open and I stuck my hand down, to slip a finger between the lips of my fanny.

Just to touch was bliss, so wonderfully relaxing that I couldn't hold back a sigh of pleasure. The lane was an empty as before and I began to masturbate, gently teasing my clit as I tried to focus on what would bring me the greatest pleasure. There was plenty to choose from, with my bottom still warm from spanking and no knickers under my shorts because I'd been made to use them to mop up my spilt tea. Yet I'd already done myself over the actual spanking, while it was the incident with Leary and Sean which had brought me to the state I was in, so turned on that I couldn't hold back from playing with myself in my car by a public road.

They thought I'd been spanked for being a naughty girl, and just that knowledge was enough to set me biting my lip and rubbing harder at the wet, eager slit between my thighs. I thought of how it might have been if Hannah had done me in front of them, which wasn't impossible, both watching with rising lust but also sympathy for my plight as I was hauled into position, my silly little shorts taken down to reveal the seat of my panties, taut and white across my cheeks, my panties taken down in turn to expose every rude detail of my rear view, my bottom pink and full and bare, the tight brown dimple of my anus, my naked cunt.

I'd shut my eyes, so high on my own shame that I no longer cared where I was, only for that appalling picture of how I'd look to them, bare and ready, fighting against the unspeakable humiliation about to be inflicted on me. Hannah would pull my top up, the way she always did, to add the exposure of my breasts to my distress. I had to be that way, and one quick tug had my top and bra up, spilling my boobs into my hands as I imagined how they'd look dangling under my chest as Leary and Sean watched me

17

being prepared for my spanking.

A quick feel and my hand was back down my panties, my fingers fiddling in my cunt as I tugged at one nipple and thought of how Hannah would spank me, not for my pleasure, but because I'd been a naughty girl. I screamed as I came, completely lost in the fantasy as my thoughts exploded into a welter of dirty possibilities, of how they might let the men masturbate over the sight of my beating, or do it all over my hot bottom while she held me down, even take turns up my cunt with their cocks in up me to the balls and their bellies pressed to my smacked cheeks.

How long my orgasm lasted I have no idea, but it finally broke to an unexpected noise from outside the car. My eyes came open and I found myself staring up in horror into the faces of the two girls I'd seen earlier, looking down on me from their horses, mouths agape and eyes wide with astonishment.

Chapter Two

Another thing about my spankings is that they help me deal with stress, usually. This time it was rather different. Being caught masturbating in my car by the two girls was hideously embarrassing, so much so that I was too ashamed of myself to enjoy my feelings, as I had with the men. Yet it was impossible to deny that there was an erotic element to what had happened, because as they'd ridden past the girls had been laughing.

If they'd been shocked, or angry, even if they'd tried to pretend nothing had happened, I would have been left feeling thoroughly ashamed of myself in a way that wasn't in the least bit sexual and eventually it would have become no more than an embarrassing but also amusing anecdote to tell my more intimate friends. As it was that moment of laughter had put a completely different complexion on things. They thought it was funny. Maybe they'd also guessed that I'd been spanked. If so, that meant they knew the truth, that I'd not only been spanked but had been so turned on by it that I'd been unable to drive more than a few yards before stopping to masturbate over what had been done to me. Worse still, like Leary and Sean, the girls had no way of knowing that I hadn't been given a real punishment.

I spent that evening in mingled self-recrimination and a state of helpless arousal I couldn't bring myself to satisfy. Kay was in Spain, sorting out the estate of an elderly uncle and while usually I hate being without her, this time I was quite glad. I tried to cope with my feelings with an old movie and a bottle of wine, but it didn't really work. By the end I was merely maudlin, but exhaustion finally caught up and rescued me instead.

By the Monday morning I was more or less back to my usual self, only without the sense of wellbeing I usually enjoy after a good spanking. That was irritating, and I even thought of closing up the shop and driving over to see Hannah for another dose. She'd have given me what I wanted, but for some reason the idea wasn't fully satisfying. It also seemed risky, for all that I knew it was my own silly fault that I'd been caught, so in the end I decided to spend the morning doing my accounts in an effort to distract myself.

I was keeping my head above water, just, but my income wasn't close to what it had been a few years before. Unfortunately it was hard to see what I could do, because although I knew I wasn't making proper use of my land it was too small to be much use for agriculture. Most of it had been old railway sidings anyway and there were areas of oil contamination, no longer visible but still a problem when it came to what I was allowed to use it for. Razorback Paintball Club came up occasionally because they knew that I would put up with their dirty habits, such as hunting girls with the seats cut out of their jeans and targets painted on their bottoms, but even they weren't using it as often as they once had, having found a larger space down on the south coast.

At the very least I could advertise, but the chances of picking anything up in the village seemed remote, so I decided to surf the net to see what else I could do. The land is an odd shape, with a paddock behind the house, the area of old sidings and a long thin stretch running beside the railway to join what used to be my godfather's land. When Henry had been alive we'd used it for all sorts of delightfully naughty goings on, but since he'd passed away

I'd rather lost heart.

I'd also lost quite a lot of my old contacts, most of them in fact, except for Morris Rathwell, who always kept in touch even if only because he liked to treat his female friends as a gigantic harem. He at least was an option, but dealing with Morris invariably came at a cost, and not one I like to pay, so I put the idea of contacting him aside as a last resort. I knew I could also strike a deal with Razorback, but again at a cost. Remembering some of the things they'd done to me – or to be entirely truthful that we'd done together – sent a shiver the length of my spine. I promised myself I'd try my best to find a less perverse option, one that didn't involve being chased half-naked through the woods, done up as an erotic clown, or made to wallow in mud in nothing but a rubber pig's snout and a curly tail.

It wasn't easy, especially as my computer didn't seem to want to behave. A lot of people seemed to be in a similar situation to my own, so that there was plenty of land available for outdoor pursuits, most of it more suitable than my own. A lot more public land had been set aside for similar purposes as well, while some of the clubs who might have wanted to rent from me had made purchases of their own. Again and again I came back to the option of calling Morris, and again and again I held back. At the very least he would expect me to attend one of his notorious spanking parties, or more likely ask to hold it at my place after the event. Being spanked by Hannah was one thing, but Morris meant men, dirty old men, and lots of them, which is another thing entirely.

I was biting my lip as I went back to surfing, thinking of old times and the way Morris had toyed with me across the years. There was no denying that I'd got a lot out of it, my house and land for one thing, or that ultimately I'd enjoyed the dirty games, for all my hurt pride. I hadn't been all that long out of school the first time he had me, on my knees in the mud with a yoke around my neck and my bottom lifted

21

for rear entry. The thought still sent a shiver of mingled excitement and shame right through me, although I'd left that part of my life behind. It had been two years since he'd last caught me out, he and his wife tricking me into taking a very public spanking, and only slightly less since I'd accepted a man's cock. Since then life had been quieter, and a lot more dignified, even allowing for my occasional spankings from Hannah.

Just to think of that last public spanking left me feeling sulky and resentful, but also nostalgic, so I called up some of my old pictures on the computer. There was a truly glorious set of me punishing Morris's wife Melody, with her full, black bottom lifted naked to the camera, her big breasts swinging bare under her chest and her face set in the most wonderful scowl of consternation for what was being done to her. Morris had taken them himself, never one to spare his wife's blushes, or any other woman's, for that matter. Another set showed her and her sister at one of the Razorback Paintball events, both with their bottoms showing bare through the cut out seats of their jeans, their dark skin splashed with coloured dye. I remembered the occasion well, and I'd been in an equally sorry state myself, but the memory still made me laugh. It was only a shame that nobody had shot Morris.

The picture had been taken on my own land, where a fair bit of landscaping and carefully tended hedges ensured our privacy and had incidentally left it rather pretty, which gave me a new idea. It would be an ideal location for a little discreet photography, or even filming, as would my stable yard. I had no idea if the idea was viable, let alone how much it would bring in, but there was no harm in trying and so I spent the next couple of hours posting adverts on suitable internet sites. In every case I had to sign up first, a tedious process, and I was still at it when the sound of the bell drew my attention to the shop.

Three women had come in, a mother and two daughters

22

by the look of them. For one ghastly moment I thought the two girls were the ones who'd caught me in the lane, but one of the few things I'd noticed about the riders was that one had bright red hair. Both these girls were dark, and probably a little younger, but they had that same air of insouciant pride, an unselfconscious poise that bordered on arrogance, as did the older woman.

All were of above average height, slender and well groomed. The eldest was in tweeds, beautifully cut and still smart but well worn, the clothes of a woman with no need to make a demonstration of her wealth or status. She looked about fifty, or possibly older but very well preserved, her features fine if a trifle angular and her expression supremely confident and a little stern as she examined my display of riding whips. Both girls carried themselves the same way, although their bodies were firmer, more buoyant, and it was impossible not to admire them. They were so close in age they might have been twins, both with small, firm breasts apparently bare under their jumpers and neatly rounded bottoms packed into tight blue jeans. One wore her hair loose, in a soft black cloud that fell to the middle of her back, while her sister had piled hers into a tight bun. They remained looking at the whips as the older woman approached the counter.

'Good morning. Do you stock a full range of equestrian prerequisites?'

I'd never heard them called that before, but hastened to assure her that I did, and could easily get hold of anything I didn't have in stock. She began to ask specific questions, and it quickly became clear that while they had stables and horses, they lacked land. It was too good an opportunity to miss.

'I have a paddock you might be interested in renting,' I offered, 'including jumps.'

'Indeed?

'Yes, I ...'

'We might consider it, should it prove suitable.'

'Of course. When would you like to look round?'

'Now will do very well. Portia, Ophelia.'

I'd been going to point out that I was alone in the shop when she turned to call to the two girls, but thought better of it as it was very nearly lunchtime in any case. Not that I was entirely sure I'd let her use the land, as her haughty, superior manner was irritating, although that in turn made me realise that Hannah and Maggie probably felt the same way about me.

The girl with her hair up had been examining an expensive crop with a horn and silver handle, and as her mother called to them she took advantage of her sister's momentary inattention to flick the end at one denim clad bottom cheek. Her victim squeaked and jumped, clutching at herself as she turned on her sister in fury.

'Ow, that hurt!'

'Do at least try and act your age, Ophelia,' the older woman sighed, 'and you too, Portia. We are going to look around.'

The one who was presumably Portia put the crop back, ignoring a glare from her sister and still wearing a distinctly smug little smile as she approached. I now realised that they weren't quite as alike as I'd first imagined. Portia was clearly older, but only by a year, if that, while Ophelia had an upturned nose and more freckles, adding a touch of the brat to her ladylike demeanour. I went to lock the door and turn the sign around before showing the three of them out through the kitchen and into the yard.

'I'm Amber Oakley, by the way,' I told them as we came outside.

'Marjorie Crowthorne-Jones,' she replied, then indicated the girls. 'My daughters, Portia and Ophelia. Ah, yes, this will be most suitable.'

'This is simply my yard, I'm afraid. Your access would be through the gate a little way down the road.'

24

'At the very least we would need use of your yard tap, and other suitable facilities.'

I found myself agreeing despite my reservations and she went on.

'I have recently purchased the Cedars. There is a stable block, but the land was sold separately, so the girls and I would certainly benefit from somewhere to practise until we can find a suitable field.'

I knew the Cedars, a large Georgian house at the far side of the village that had been on the market for some time and needed a lot of work. Evidently the Crowthorne-Joneses were comfortably off if not actually wealthy. The arrangement seemed ideal, for all her superior manner, and I found myself eager to impress as I led them through to the paddock. It had been a while since I'd painted the jumps, and I was sure she gave a faint sniff as she saw, but it was Portia who spoke up.

'This will do, although it's not very large.'

'You can use the Old Siding as well,' I pointed out, gesturing to where the path led away between twin hedges, 'and there's what I call the Strip beyond, which runs for two miles alongside the railway. There's a made-up path.'

'I see.'

The girls had already moved off to one side and were giggling over some private joke, which I had a nasty suspicion was at my expense. Again I wondered if one of them, more likely Portia, hadn't been the dark haired girl who'd caught me, perhaps with a red haired friend, but it was impossible to be sure and I could hardly ask her. As we started across the paddock they ran ahead, full of energy and quickly disappearing beyond the hedges. It had been a while since I'd used the land for anything rude and I was fairly sure I'd cleared up all the potentially incriminating bits and pieces, but it was impossible not to feel nervous, especially when a clear, silvery laugh carried back from ahead.

'This is all old railway land,' I explained to Mrs

Crowthorne-Jones, 'and there was some oil contamination, which limits its use, a lot of rubble too, which is how I made these banks.'

'I see.'

Something in her tone of voice suggested that this was a socially embarrassing admission to be making and I quickly went on, suddenly and irrationally determined to show her that I was more than simply one of the local tradespeople.

'My main reason for buying it was to make sure it didn't get built over. There are quite enough houses in the village as it is.'

'Oh, absolutely.'

Her positive response brought me a flush of pleasure, immediately followed by annoyance at myself. It was like being back at school again, desperate to please my latest crush among the teachers, which was ridiculous at my age. We'd reached the open area beyond the alley of hedges, scene of so much lewd behaviour. I found myself glancing around in apprehension, but even the paintball splats had long ago washed away, and although she might well have disapproved there would have been nothing to suggest that the targets were girls with the bottoms cut out of their jeans. I resolved to make a thorough search anyway, for anything even as mildly suspicious as a discarded pair of panties.

I was wondering what had happened to Portia and Ophelia when they emerged from the building we used as a changing room, once more making me apprehensive. Both were laughing, but again it seemed to be at some private joke, possibly at my expense. I found myself pursing my lips in irritation and tried to restore my equilibrium by imagining them playing in one of the paintball games, with their little round bottoms peeping out where the material of their skinny jeans had been cut away, bare and vulnerable as they waited for the game to start or bouncing cheekily behind them as they ran.

'It's a bit of a dump,' Portia stated as they reached us,

'but it'll do.'

'Yes,' Ophelia agreed, 'it'll do, as long as we can use it whenever we like.'

'That would depend …' I began, only to be interrupted by Portia.

'You'll get your money, but I can't be bothered with having to book times or anything like that. Is that clear?'

'I'm sure Miss Oakley appreciates our requirements,' her mother put in before I could think of a response other than putting the little brat straight across my knee, 'but yes, constant access is essential, so we will of course require a key.'

'To the gate, yes,' I responded, desperately trying to regain control over the situation, 'but we haven't discussed the rent.'

'I don't think that will prove to be a difficulty,' she said, reaching for her handbag.

'I was thinking, perhaps …'

'You are to have the jumps painted and the grass cut,' she stated, interrupting me in a tone so sure her words came across more as an order than a request, or even a simple statement of fact, as if no other option were conceivable.

My mouth came open to protest, more for her attitude than what she was suggesting, which was reasonable enough, but she had taken a sheath of notes from her bag, which she held out to me as she carried on and I bit back my words.

'A month in advance. Your hedges could also do with trimming, and the whole area with tidying up a little.'

I barely heard her demands. She was offering at least twice as much as I'd intended to ask, maybe more, and I was trying to not to seem too eager as I took the money.

'I'll make you out a receipt,' I offered.

Ten minutes later they were gone, leaving me with distinctly mixed feelings. On the one hand I'd managed to rent out the land, and at a good price, but on the other I found their attitude exasperating. They were sure to be hard work, with constant demands for this and that. Again I wondered whether I made Hannah and Maggie feel the same way, which led me to some pleasant speculation about what I'd do if only I was able to deal with the Crowthorne-Joneses the same way the travellers dealt with me. All three of them would definitely have benefited from a good spanking, all the more so if Portia really was one of the girls who'd caught me, because to give her a dose of what she found so amusing would have been immensely satisfying.

It was still lunchtime, so I made myself a sandwich and poured a glass of wine before putting my feet up in the kitchen and letting my imagination roam. My feelings of shame for the way I'd been caught were still there, but no longer strong enough to stop me enjoying my fantasy. I would spank them in front of each other, Ophelia first, as I'd now learnt for certain that she was the youngest for all that she looked like a twin to her big sister. A hand spanking would be sufficient, over my knee with her beautiful little bottom straining out the seat of her jeans, at least at first. That way I could let her think she'd be allowed to stay clothed, only to be told that the spanking wasn't having enough effect on her and that her jeans had to come down.

She'd make a fuss, but I wouldn't take any nonsense, holding her tightly in place as I tugged the jeans low to show off the seat of her panties. They'd probably be quite fancy, a designer label for sure, perhaps silk with a wide lace trim, tight enough to show off every contour of her sweet little rump. I'd play the same game with her once more, spanking her for a while before telling her that I was going to have to pull down her panties.

This time she'd make a real fuss, far more than she had over her jeans. Maybe she'd even fight, wriggling on my lap and clutching at her panties in a desperate effort to keep them up. I'd merely tighten my grip, twisting her arm into the small of her back as I peeled the tiny garment down to expose her perfect little bottom, the rounded cheeks firm and high, parted a little to show the sweetly turned split of her fanny and the tight dimple of her anus. All of it would be in full view of her mother and sister, who'd watch with mounting horror as the spanking began, with some concern for what was happening to Ophelia but a great deal more because they'd know they were next.

I shook myself and glanced at my watch. The temptation to slip a hand down my panties was close to irresistible, and yet in a few minutes I was supposed to open the shop and there was a delivery due for the early afternoon. Maybe if I was quick I could just manage it, a thought that brought me a flush of shame for the memory of the last time I'd done it. Yet now I was safe, and with that thought my fingers were fumbling at the button of my jeans. It came open, my zip slipped down and my fingers were in my knickers, on the warm, silky mound of my fanny, then delving into the wet slit between my lips. As I began to masturbate I'd closed my eyes, imagining the scene, Ophelia now standing against the wall with her hands on her head and her red bottom on show to the room as I called her sister forward.

Portia would know she had no chance of being permitted the dignity of keeping her clothes up, so there would be no point in playing games with her. I'd make her stand in front of me while I took down her jeans and panties instead, baring her bottom and fanny before she even went over my knee. Having seen how ridiculous her sister looked struggling and kicking as she was spanked she'd try and be cool about it, determined not to give me the satisfaction of seeing her react to her exposure and pain.

Her composure wouldn't last. No sooner would her perfect little bottom be stuck high with her bumhole and fanny lips on show than she'd be sobbing, and it would only take a few firm smacks to have her gasping and kicking her legs. Once the spanking got going she'd lose her dignity completely, begging me to stop and promising never to be cheeky again as she squirmed and bucked to the stinging slaps. I'd show no mercy, spanking her until she was as red behind as her sister and then sending her to stand against the wall in the same shameful position.

I was nearly there, my pleasure coming in waves as I teased my clitoris, my need too high to be denied. Another glance at my watch showed that I'd almost certainly be OK, and I paused to pull up my top and bra, spilling my breasts into my hands to stroke my erect nipples and squeeze at my flesh before returning to my fantasy. It was harder to get my head around the idea of punishing Mrs Crowthorne-Jones herself, as if even to think about such a thing was an act of impertinence so gross that the only possible response was for me to suffer the same fate as I'd just imagined dishing out to her daughters.

It was all too easy to picture. Her refusal to accept what was coming to her, a few angry words, a scuffle, and me upended across her knee, yelling indignant threats which she'd completely ignore as she stripped my bottom and got to work on me in front of the now giggling girls. It wasn't going to work though, not as a fantasy. She was no Hannah Riley, to put me across her knee by main force, and no woman is strong enough to make me submit by the force of her personality alone.

Another quick adjustment to push down my jeans and panties and I'd sat my bare bottom on the chair, my thighs now well spread and my fingers busy with my fanny and one aching nipple. Again I closed my eyes, trying to imagine how Mrs Crowthorne-Jones would take her punishment, and I suddenly I had it. I wouldn't spank her at all. I'd make Portia and Ophelia do it, sitting opposite each other with their legs interlocked, their hot little bottoms still bare on the cool wood as they took their mother across their knees, tugged up her fine tweed skirt and the slip beneath, pulled down her panties …

I came, unable to hold back any longer. My teeth were

clamped hard against my lower lip to stop myself screaming as my fingers worked furiously on my open cunt, snatching again and again at the tiny, agonisingly sensitive bud of my clitoris. It seemed to last for ever, my whole body tense as I played the scene over and over in my mind, picturing the outrage on Mrs Crowthorne-Jones's face as she was ordered to take a spanking from her own daughters, as she was bent down across their knees, as her knickers were taken down and her trim little cheeks were exposed to view, and as she was spanked and spanked and spanked, mercilessly hard by the two shamefaced girls.

Chapter Three

It was only a fantasy, but it was a good one, and all the more satisfying over the next few days. They proved even more demanding than I'd expected, first criticising my hedge trimming, which I'd completed in a single morning by borrowing a tractor with a specialised cutter from a neighbouring farmer, and then demanding that I paint the stripes on the jumps in red, blue and green, according to some system I'd never heard of. By the time I'd finished I could cheerfully have strangled them, never mind spanked them, but I was at least grateful for their casual attitude to our agreement. With no formal contract I could rent the land out for whatever other purposes I liked, and by the end of the week some of my internet postings were beginning to bear fruit.

The Crowthorne-Joneses clearly had priority, but they seemed to have a fairly predictable routine. Marjorie Crowthorne-Jones herself would arrive first thing in the morning, sometimes before I was awake, to go hacking along the Strip and possibly try out one or two jumps. She rode well, very straight and elegant in her saddle, and clearly had a lifetime of experience behind her. The girls were nearly as good, and had presumably been riding since early childhood, as they could cope with jumps I'd have thought twice about tackling and would race each other along the strip at breakneck speed. They were also very smart, in polished black riding boots, corduroy jodhpurs and tailored black jackets over white blouses, more as if they were in a competition than simply out for practise and exercise. Occasionally their mother would join them in the afternoon, putting them through their paces on the jumps and generally being bossy, which seemed to come naturally to all three of them.

Their routine meant that there was nobody about for around six hours in the middle of the day and after seven o'clock or so in the evening, so I was happy to accept a photographic booking for two hours after noon on the Friday. The photographer arrived on time, the model a few minutes late. He was a friendly if slightly seedy-looking man who paid in cash and introduced himself simply as Dave, while she was a woman of about my own age, more handsome than pretty but with striking chestnut hair and a slim, well toned body.

They accepted a cup of tea, disappeared out to the Old Siding for two hours and returned, Dave now looking pleased with himself. I wasn't entirely sure what they'd got up to, but it wasn't any of my business as long as they hadn't left any mess. A quick inspection revealed no more than a few scrape marks in the ground and I returned to the house satisfied with the situation. If anything it was easier money than renting to the Crowthorne-Joneses, although not so reliable.

I was also sure the Crowthorne-Joneses could be trusted. The girls might have been brats but I could hardly imagine them as petty thieves, while for their mother it would have been unthinkable. That didn't mean I was going to give them the run of my house, as there were some things I definitely did not want them to see, but by the middle of the second week I was sharing coffee with Marjorie in the mornings. She was always very reserved in her manner, but at least accepted me as an equal. With the girls it was another matter, as they didn't seem capable of accepting me as anything other than a menial, not only expecting me to help them with their horses and keep the jumps in good

33

order, but to bring them out tea and even toast. The good side was that I quickly became convinced that the dark girl who'd caught me masturbating wasn't Portia, if only because she was so full of smart remarks that it was impossible to imagine her holding back a comment.

Given their attitude, I was surprised when Portia asked if I'd like to watch them compete in the Bayden gymkhana. I'd been planning to go anyway and accepted, only to find that the real reason they wanted me there was so that I could drive some of their gear over as their mother wasn't around. Once there, they did at least come across to speak to me while I was buying myself some strawberries and cream, and were really quite friendly, but hung around only long enough to introduce me to a James Sebastian, a tall man with the face of a genial fox, or possibly a distinctly upper-crust rat. I've never been particularly good at small talk and as they walked away I was once more wishing that I could take the pair of them across my knee. It wouldn't just have been for the pleasure of punishing them either. They were dressed to the nines, in skin-tight, cream-coloured jodhpurs and tailored black hunting jackets, each with the tuck of her bottom peeping out from beneath the hem, ideal spanking material. My companion also seemed to appreciate the view, allowing his gaze to linger on their retreating figures until they were hidden from view among the crowd and only then turning back to me to respond to some random and faintly embarrassed comment I'd made about the weather.

'Marvellous, yes. Do let me pay for those, and may I buy you a Pimms?'

I accepted, and was quickly given an enormous plastic cup of the stuff, along with my strawberries. That meant sitting down, and inevitably in his company, but if I was finding conversation awkward he had no such difficulty, chatting away merrily and managing to drop carefully judged compliments into the conversation at every opportunity. I'd never met such an obvious cad, with the

34

possible exception of Morris Rathwell, but James Sebastian was amusing, and generous, insisting on standing me another Pimms before we walked over to watch Portia and Ophelia compete in the dressage competition.

They were good, if not the best, and I found myself judging each as she rode and thinking of advice I could give her to improve her performance, and perhaps her respect for me, until the last competitor rode out. Not that she was particularly good, or particularly well turned out, but she did have brilliant copper-coloured hair and large glasses with thick, black frames. The last time I'd seen her I'd had my boobs out and my hand down my shorts. My mouth came open and I shut it again hastily, but I couldn't stop the blood rushing to my face as my embarrassment surged up once more and I was barely aware of James Sebastian asking me a question.

' … to the Fox and Hounds for a spot of lunch?'

'Yes, that would be very kind, thank you.'

I'd answered without thinking, and knowing only that I very definitely did not want to be at the gymkhana. The girl was bound to see me, and if she was riding in the same event she probably knew Portia and Ophelia. They'd start to talk about me, and if they were close enough she would tell them what had happened, what she'd seen, and worse if she'd noticed my red bottom cheeks and realised what had been done to me. To think of Portia and Ophelia knowing I got spanked was unbearable. Not even the Fox and Hounds was safe. The girls might come over, perhaps all three of them. I could just picture it, the red-head giggling and Portia and Ophelia reacting in shock and disgust but also delight as their friend described how I'd looked, running about with my smacked bottom on show and then frigging myself off by the road side.

'Would you prefer the Golden Lion in Southaw?' I suggested.

'And why not?' he answered, and chuckled.

35

My mind was so jumbled it took me an instant to realise that he thought I was suggesting a liaison, but that was the least of my problems. If he made a pass at me I would make some excuse, or simply decline politely. What mattered was that the red-haired girl didn't see me, and that meant not being in Bayden. I'd already turned from the ropes, and hurried on towards the area where the cars were parked, only to slow down as I realised that he might misinterpret my haste. He certainly seemed pleased with himself, and I wasn't at all sure about driving after two large measures of Pimms, so when he steered me towards an open-topped Morgan I didn't resist.

A few minutes later we were in the Golden Lion and I allowed myself to relax a little. It was the better pub, while if he had any predatory intentions towards me then he clearly believed in eating first, and at leisure. He insisted on having starters, and when we'd finished our main courses a pudding as well, with which he ordered me a glass of dessert wine while abstaining himself.

During our drive and the meal I'd learnt that he was newly retired after a career in the City and lived just outside Hatfield. Otherwise he'd focussed the conversation on me, which was a little awkward as I don't like to admit that I live with another woman on short acquaintance, so I'd simply told him there was no Mr Oakley, avoiding the truth without actually lying. He'd been a perfect gentleman throughout, but as he returned his spoon to his now empty plate of profiteroles and sat back with a knowing grin I realised the time had come for me to decline whatever proposition he was about to make. We were in the garden and had lingered long after most of the other customers had left, so he made no effort to keep his voice down as he spoke.

'Please don't think me rude, but I believe you and I have a mutual appreciation for the ah … English vice?'

My carefully chosen rebuttal died on my lips, and my shock and surprise must have shown on my face, because he

36

chuckled and shrugged, then went on.

'You're embarrassed, how charming. But seriously, it's not everybody who appreciates the joy of a well-smacked bottom, and I am something of a connoisseur of the subject, though I say so myself. So perhaps …?'

He left the question unfinished, raising his eyebrows in hope and more than a touch of amusement for my consternation. I made to speak, an angry denial, then realised it was pointless. He obviously knew the truth.

'How did you find out?'

Again he chuckled, and tapped one bony finger along the side of his nose as he answered me.

'Now that would be telling, and I don't really see that it matters in any case. What does matter is that you enjoy having your bottom smacked, and you do have a magnificent bottom, by the way, well deserving of the treatment, which I am just the man to give you.'

Clearly he didn't know everything, or if he did he was ignoring inconvenient details, both my preference for women and for dishing it out, but he did know I took it. I was blushing hot and didn't know what to say, while I was earnestly wishing I hadn't worn quite such tight jeans. They showed my bottom off to perfection, which was fine even knowing that there would be people about who'd look, even want to touch or smack me, but not when they actually suggested a spanking.

He sat back in his chair, calmly waiting for me to work through my confusion and embarrassment, no doubt to the point at which I realised that his proposal made sense, swallowed my pride and accepted. I was determined I wouldn't but I needed to find out how he knew about me. If Portia or Ophelia knew from the red-haired girl and had told him that meant it was already all over the district, but I couldn't see them having that sort of conversation with him, a man twice their age if not more. I couldn't see him speaking to Hannah either, and she wouldn't have given my

37

secret away, not to a man like him. It was far more likely that he knew Morris Rathwell or somebody from that set, who were perfectly capable of telling a friend or even a client who happened to live near me that under the right circumstances I might accept a spanking. Yet it was Portia and Ophelia who'd introduced him to me.

'Take your time,' he said casually, 'no rush, and if you'd rather keep your jeans up or anything, this first time, that's not a problem.'

I shook my head, unable even to begin to cope with the sheer arrogance of his statement, which implied not only that I was going to let him spank me, but that even if he condescended to let me keep my jeans up this time, then on the next occasion I'd be done bare whether I liked it or not. Yet his words had sent a shiver through me and I found myself pursing my mouth in annoyance for my own treacherous feelings. Once more he chuckled, then spoke again.

'Let me guess then. You're rather shy about going bare? Maybe you prefer the choice taken out of your hands?'

The blood rushed up to my face in a hot wave. Maybe he was guessing, but more likely he knew, and that meant Portia and Ophelia had nothing to do with it. At most they knew I got it and liked it, but no such rude details. Relief swept through me and I found myself smiling despite my blushes.

'Morris told you, didn't he?' I said.

For an instant Sebastian looked puzzled, then once more tapped the side of his nose.

'Melody?' I asked. 'Penny?'

Now he looked shifty.

'I promised not to say, and I am a man of my word, as you will discover should you choose to submit your delectable bottom to my ministrations.'

There was something not quite right, but my overwhelming emotion was still relief. I decided to let him down gently.

'The thing is, James, I really prefer women.'

'No wriggling, young lady,' he answered. 'I think we both know what you prefer.'

'No, really …'

I stopped. He was being firm with me, playing the dominant male, which put my back up but always made the subsequent punishment that much better when I did give in. It had been nearly two weeks since my session with Hannah, much of it spent admiring the Crowthorne-Joneses' beautifully pert bottoms. His attitude and just talking about spanking was putting me off balance as well, and I'd carried on before I could stop myself.

'OK, just a few across the seat of my jeans, if you must, but with an implement.'

'As you wish.'

Now there was no mistaking the firm, commanding tone in his voice. I was shaking as he went inside to pay, cursing myself for being so weak-willed and desperately trying to find excuses for my behaviour: that a few cuts with a cane or something across the seat of my jeans would leave him more frustrated than anything, that is was a necessary sacrifice to keep him quiet about my penchant for spanking, even that it was only fair to give him what he wanted when he'd bought me an expensive lunch. None of it was true. I wanted my bottom beaten.

When he came back out he simply extended his hand, not speaking. I took it and let him lead me away, trailing behind him as we went, only not to his car but into the dark mouth of a footpath where it opened from the woods beside the pub. It made sense, if he was only going to give me a quick whipping, but we were only a couple of miles from my house and I did not want a repeat of the incident with the two riders.

'Well into the woods, please,' I asked.

'Naturally,' he responded. 'We wouldn't want anybody

39

to see what you get, would we? That's just between you and me, isn't it?'

'Yes,' I agreed and meant it.

It had been a long time since a man had done anything sexual with me, and I was having enough trouble coming to terms with it myself, never mind having anybody else know, but I'd given in and let him lead me as we made our way ever deeper into the woods. When we did stop we were well off the footpath, in an overgrown area of hornbeam and oak, untended and even free of litter, a sure sign that we'd be undisturbed. One of the big trees had come down and we found ourselves a space beside the main trunk, completely sheltered from view, where I turned and hung my head, ready to accept what we'd agreed on.

'What a good girl you are,' he said. 'It's not your first time, we both know that, but tell me, how many men, and women, have punished you?'

'I don't know,' I admitted.

'You don't know?' he queried, laughing. 'Well if that isn't a good reason to whip you I don't know what is! Right then, lean your hands on the tree trunk, feet together, bottom well raised. That's right, good girl. You do have experience, don't you?'

I'd got into the humiliating position he'd demanded, presenting my jeans-clad bottom for his attention, meanwhile wondering just how many people had spanked or beaten me over the years. It was an embarrassingly high number, certainly above fifty, maybe even a hundred, my bottom presented for punishment again and again, just as it was now.

He'd gone to find himself something to beat me with, but I knew I was supposed to hold my position to add to my feelings of shame and did so without having to be told. Even when I saw what he'd chosen I didn't flinch, but it was impossible to resist biting my lip. The fallen oak had brought down a smaller tree, a wild plum, from the base of which long, flexible shoots had sprung up, just right for making a switch that would not only hurt but leave marks on my flesh even through my jeans.

I watched in rising apprehension as he took out a pocket knife and cut not one, but three of the shoots. Each was about four feet long and as thick as one of my fingers at the base, also whippy and green with sap. It was going to hurt, a lot, and I found myself wishing I'd been less prissy about keeping my jeans up and opted to go bare bottom over his knee instead, which might have been more intimate and humiliating but would be a great deal less painful. He was in no hurry either, carefully plaiting the three shoots together and using twists of rough grass to bind the tip and base. Satisfied, he gave the horrid little thing, a couple of experimental swishes through the air and then walked back to me, grinning.

'Just the thing for a big girl like you, isn't it?' he said, holding out the switch for my inspection. 'After all, just because you get to keep your modesty doesn't mean the punishment should be diluted, does it? No, it doesn't. Rather the opposite, in fact, don't you agree?'

He laughed as I shook my head, then tapped the switch across the seat of my jeans. I shut my eyes, struggling to keep my breathing even as I waited, wondering what the hell I was doing in the depths of a wood with my bottom stuck out for some bastard to beat me but at the same time knowing that if I backed out now I'd end up desperately frustrated. A sob escaped my mouth as he continued to hold off and I glanced back, just as he brought the switch down across my bottom. It hurt crazily, a hot, stinging pain that had me jumping on my toes and clutching at my cheeks. I was out of practice, particularly with stinging implements, and I'd forgotten how much it hurt, but that didn't stop me getting back in my rude, receptive position as soon as I was able.

'Good girl,' he remarked and gave me a second.

Again I jumped up, gasping and rubbing at myself, and again he allowed me to regain my composure and get back into position without comment. He was grinning though, plainly enjoying himself and I was cursing him under my breath even as I stuck my bottom out for more. The next was harder still, and lower, to leave a burning line full across the tuck of my cheeks once I'd finished my silly little dance of pain.

'You are well-behaved, aren't you?' he remarked as I once more presented myself. 'But I can't help but think that you're getting rather more out of this than I am, no?'

I gave my head an angry shake, or what was supposed to be an angry shake, because of course he was right. There were now three hot lines across my rear cheeks, sending the heat to my fanny, but while he was no doubt enjoying beating me and also the sight of my out-thrust bottom, that only went so far. After all, he could have admired the way I filled the seat of my jeans at the gymkhana.

'OK, if you have to be such a pervert,' I told him, 'you can have me bare.'

I'd unfastened my jeans as I spoke, and quickly pushed them down, taking my panties with them to show him my bare bottom. There was no denying that it felt right, and my flesh was already decorated with three thin red lines where the switch had caught me. He merely nodded, accepting his right to have my jeans and knickers down as his due, but he stepped behind me to get a peep at my fanny before once more tapping the cane to my bottom.

'Very pretty,' he remarked, and once more brought the switch down across my flesh.

If it had hurt on my jeans, then on my bare flesh it was agony. I screamed and jumped up, kicking and dancing as I squeezed my burning flesh, calling him a bastard over and over again, but when I finally regained control I stuck my bottom out higher still. This time I could see the lust in his eyes as he once more steadied the switch across my bottom, while the bulge where his trousers hid his cock was noticeably bigger than it had been. The thought of cock sent another sharp thrill through me, followed by shame, for the way I was flaunting myself for a man, for my submission, but most of all because I very definitely did not want to stop.

The switch cracked down again, biting into my flesh to set me jumping and clutching at my bottom one more time, but I was soon back in position. Again he took aim, again he brought the switch down across my cheeks, and again, each stroke making me dance and leaving a fresh welt across the pale skin of my bottom, a mark to show not only what had been done to me but what I was, a whipped girl, knickers down in the woods for a man's pleasure.

I pulled out my own tits, between strokes, fumbling the buttons of my blouse open and shrugging it off, then taking off my bra to leave myself topless, more ashamed of myself than ever, and more excited. He gave an appreciative nod for my display, but said nothing, merely tapping the switch on the tree trunk to indicate that I should get back in position. I obeyed, and as I pushed out my bottom once more I caught the scent of my own sex, rich with arousal. He was no less turned on, his cock now a rigid bar beneath the material of his trousers, ready for the wet hole between my thighs, just as my hole was ready for him, but not my head.

'You're not to fuck me,' I said urgently, yet my words were an admission that it was at least a possibility and I hastily went on. 'Seriously, I haven't any protection, but … but you can do it over my bottom if you want to.'

My voice was thick with embarrassment as I spoke, and he hadn't even made a move to get his cock out, but we both knew it was going to happen. The pretence was over, my bottom bare, my fanny wet and ready, showing my excitement for what was being done to me and what might be yet to come. He raised the switch, brought it down and again I yelped with pain as it bit into my flesh, but stayed in position. Another cut followed in quick succession, and a third, to leave me stamping my feet in the leaf litter and sobbing with reaction, but still ready. He paused and I glanced at him, wondering if he was ready to pull out his cock and take me up on my lewd offer. As he saw where my eyes were directed he gave a pleased chuckle, then spoke again.

'Up on your toes, let's have your bumhole showing.'

'No, really … oh God!'

I'd done it, unable to resist his words, lifting myself onto my toes to make my cheeks spread and show off the tight brown ring of my anus as well as my fanny lips. He came close, inspecting me from a distance of just inches, then ran one finger gently across my skin, tracing the line of a welt to where it faded at the edge of my slit, and deeper, to tickle my anus and make the little ring contract.

'What a rude bottom hole you have,' he said, 'pink in the middle with a brown ring, and so prettily puckered, like a little mouth.'

He was still touching, his finger tracing the outline of my bumhole as he spoke, to set me treading my feet in the dirt and sobbing with reaction, the tears welling in my eyes as I began to cry. At that he stopped and bent down, peering into my face.

'Don't stop,' I told him. 'Beat me, punish me.'

In answer he stood up, to leave his crotch level with my face. His fingers went to his zip and I realised he was going to make me suck his cock but even as I shook my head in mute protest my mouth had come open. He sensed my distress and began to stroke my hair as he pulled down his zip, speaking as he rummaged in his pants to free his erection.

'There, there, I'm sure this won't be the first cock in your mouth, nor the last. Now suck it.'

His cock was out, big and pale, the head already glossy with pressure and the hole at the tip wet with his excitement. The tears were rolling down my cheeks and my vision was a blur as his grip tightened in my hair, pulling me forward and on to his erection. I took it in, my mouth filling with the taste of man as I began to suck cock for the first time in what seemed like an age. His hand found my bottom again as I sucked, feeling my welts and the meat of my cheeks before sliding between to tickle my anus. I'd guessed he liked girl's bottoms from the start, when I'd seen him admiring the turn of Portia's and Ophelia's cheeks in their jodhpurs, and wondered if his desire extended to sticking his cock up our bumholes.

'Aren't you tight, so very tight,' he sighed, confirming my fears.

I shook my head but he merely chuckled, then moved his hand, cupping my fanny as I continued to suck on his erection. He'd put down the switch, but I was wishing he could do everything at once, beat me while I sucked his cock and masturbate me at the same time. Not that I needed more beating, my bottom already stripy with welts and as hot as I could possibly have wished. I thought he was going to spunk in my mouth anyway, but he'd suddenly pulled back, leaving his cock and balls rearing in front of my face for a moment before he stepped behind me once more.

'You first,' he said. 'How would you like it?'

He was still rubbing my cunt, hard enough to send shivers of pleasure through me and set me gasping as I struggled to answer.

'Whip me … whip me while you do it.'

He nodded and picked up the switch. I braced my feet apart, as far as my jeans and panties would permit me, leant my weight on the trunk of the oak and stuck my bottom high. I was spread, cunt and anus on offer to a man's hand, and his whip, his cock too if he chose to stick it up me, because he'd have been in before I could protest. When he took his erection in his hand I thought he was going to do it, even try and force it up my bum, but all I could manage in protest was a weak sob, which broke to a cry of pain as the switch lashed down across my cheeks.

I was gasping and wriggling as he beat me, lashing the switch down across my already tortured bottom as he masturbated, harder and harder until I was screaming in pain. Only then did he step in close, his hand cupping my ready cunt to rub hard in my slit as he continued to whip my bottom, bringing the switch down on the top of my cheeks again and again, to welt what little flesh he'd spared before. I was screaming my head off, the tears running so hard they spattered on the wood beneath my face, but I was coming, his fingers working my clit to perfection even as he thrashed me.

My vision went red as I started to come, my screams broke to choking sobs and my legs gave way, to leave me slumped across the tree trunk, my bottom still stuck high, his fingers still busy with my cunt as wave after wave of ecstasy ran through me. He never stopped, thrashing at my bottom with the switch and rubbing at my slit until at last I could take no more and was begging him to stop. His hand left my cunt but he carried on beating me and I realised he was masturbating over my bottom as he thrashed me an instant before hot, wet spunk spattered out across my burning cheeks and into the slit between. At the thought of having my anus wet with spunk a final shiver ran through me and it was over, my cunt frigged to ecstasy, my bottom well and truly thrashed, then spunked on.

Chapter Four

My whipping from James Sebastian left me on a glorious high. I hadn't realised how badly I'd needed sex, or not so much sex as sexual interaction. There was guilt too, because for all that Kay and I aren't exclusive I knew that she'd be surprised and shocked that I'd given in to a man, and that my excuse, that I'd held back from letting him fuck me, was pretty thin. For one thing I knew perfectly well that if he'd put his cock up me at the very end I wouldn't have resisted, and might even have tried to accommodate him up my bottom.

There's a wonderful irony about feeling guilty over taking a punishment though, because there's no better way to deal with it than another punishment. I felt I needed one, really quite badly, but it was going to have to wait. My bottom was criss-crossed with welts, and while it was more than I could resist to pull my panties down and admire my rear view in the mirror at every opportunity I was definitely going to have to recover before letting anybody else have another go with me. That included James Sebastian, although he had made it very plain as we walked back through the woods that he would enjoy another session. I had explained how things stood with Kay and that he shouldn't expect too much, a situation he'd accepted with about as much reluctance as you'd expect of a man offered the chance of regular sex with no strings.

I knew that in many eyes that would make me a slut, so I was careful to swear him to secrecy and extremely glad when no mention was made of our abrupt departure from the gymkhana. There didn't seem to be any repercussions from the presence of the red-haired girl either, or at least when Portia and Ophelia rode over for practice the following day their behaviour was no different from usual, arrogant and demanding but with none of the giggles and shocked looks I'd have expected if they'd known what the other girl knew. I still didn't feel secure, but there was nothing I could do beyond keeping myself to myself rather more than usual and parking the car in the yard instead of the street in case she happened to come past and recognise it rather than me.

On the Monday morning I took my second booking from a photographer, a man calling himself Litenshade but soon revealed as a Mr Antrobus. He was full of questions about my land, how secluded it was and whether I minded him taking nude studies, while my efforts to reassure him only seemed to make him more shifty and insecure. It was amusing at first but quickly grew irritating, especially as my computer was still playing up, as if it was pausing to think about what to do next every time I needed to use a different application.

His attitude was a striking contrast to James, who had called me the next day to enquire after the condition of my bottom and suggest another rendezvous. He had no qualms whatsoever about what we'd done, chuckling over my description of the welts that decorated my cheeks and then calling again the next day to suggest that I drive over and show him, followed by a leisurely dinner. I agreed, but made him promise not to spank me, which made him laugh.

He was as good as his word, but when I turned up in a skirt and no knickers, both to spare my welts and make it easier to show off to him, he made me pin the hem up at the back to leave my bottom showing. It was a classic gesture, shameful and rude, so much so that my intentions of holding back dissolved completely over the skilfully made pasta and the bottle of Chianti he served. He had me kneel for him, my skirt still up and my boobs pulled out as I sucked on his cock, like a teenage tart after a successful dinner date, and really there wasn't that much difference.

Twice during the evening I tried to get him to tell me how he'd knew I liked to be spanked. Once again he refused, and once again he pointed out that if I expected him to keep my secrets then I could hardly expect him to reveal other people's.It was impossible to argue with that, but the next morning I called Morris. He denied knowing anybody called James Sebastian and didn't seem to recognise my description, but I wasn't convinced, having long ago learnt never to accept anything Morris Rathwell did or said at its face value. I even wondered if there wasn't some complicated scheme afoot, no doubt intended to end with me tarred and feathered or used as the plaything for a hundred or so perverts, but in the end decided that I was just being paranoid.

At lunchtime on the following day a letter arrived, with a local postmark but otherwise completely plain, no signature, no hint as to who it was from, but I didn't need to be told. It bore a simple message – "In your workshop, Friday 9pm, nude, on all fours, saddled up." In the circumstances, only James could have sent it, which meant he knew even more than I'd suspected, not only about my taste for spanking, but also about the games I like to play. That in turn made it almost certain that it was Morris who'd told him, and if there were one or two alternatives that made no difference. He knew, he wanted to be part of it, and I wasn't going to resist.

I could have done, pointing out once more that he was the wrong sex and that I preferred to be in charge, but it would have just seemed petty. After all, I'd enjoyed my whipping and I'd enjoyed playing the tart for him. The boundaries of our relationship were established, with me on the bottom, and just so long as it remained our secret that was fine. The thought of what he'd demanded was enough to leave me trembling as well. I'd be waiting for him in my workshop, nude but for a bridle and a saddle on my back so that he could ride me like an animal. It was a fantasy I'd enjoyed since I'd first begun to explore my sexuality, usually as the rider or trainer, but being put in harness myself often enough. I'd gone too long without it.

Mr Antrobus was booked for the Friday evening at seven o'clock, but only for one hour, which he'd explained would enable to him to get the best of the evening light, so while it was annoying it wasn't really a problem. As it was he arrived early, but shortly after Portia and Ophelia had left, to my relief. He was a small man in late middle age, every bit as shifty as his emails had led me to imagine, but I had little choice but to invite him in for a cup of tea, while apparently his model wasn't due until the proper time.

'I would like to inspect the location,' he told me, his eyes flicking between my chest and hips as he blew on his tea to cool it down, 'if you wouldn't mind showing me around?'

He had a peculiar voice, a high, petulant whine, but oddly determined, as if he was about to launch into a long and complicated explanation of something at any moment. I found it irritating, but not as much as the way he kept undressing me with his eyes, so that I knew full well that in his head I had my boobs out and my jeans and knickers around my ankles, all on show for his personal inspection. Not that he was dangerous, being several inches shorter than me for one thing, but just having him in my house was highly embarrassing. Outside wasn't much better, but at least I'd have something to do rather than putting up with half-an-hour of feeling awkward while I tried to make conversation.

'Delilah89 will call me when she arrives,' he said, showing me his mobile phone.

It took me an instant to realise that Delilah89 had to be the name his model used on the net, and it still seemed a weird way to refer to her, unless she hadn't given him her real name at all.

'You're very welcome to shoot anywhere you like,' I told him as we entered the paddock, 'except in the house, of course.'

'And it's not overlooked?' he asked.

'No,' I assured him, although I'd already said so several times during our exchange of emails.

He didn't seem to believe me anyway, making a careful circuit of the paddock and trying to peer over the hedges before returning to where I was waiting.

'And I can use the show jumps?' he asked.

'Yes,' I told him, 'and this area …'

I stopped. I'd heard the rattle of chain and a moment later Portia's clear, silvery laugh followed.

'The jumps, yes,' I said hastily, 'er …'

'Do we have company?' he asked.

'Two girls who ride on my land,' I explained. 'I thought they'd gone home.'

I'd meant to shepherd him away from the girls, but it was already too late. Portia's horse nosed around the end of the hedges on the banks, closely followed by her sister, and we were forced to step aside to let them pass.

'Good evening, fair maidens,' Mr Antrobus remarked, making me cringe.

Portia looked down at him as if he was something particularly unpleasant she'd found on the bottom of her shoe but didn't bother to reply, addressing me instead.

'Mother's entertaining,' she said, 'so we're going to practise for a while.'

'Of course,' I replied, too flustered to argue, 'if you could come this way, Mr Antrobus, please?'

Portia and Ophelia had ridden on, not even bothering to glance back, and to my immense relief Mr Antrobus did as I'd asked and followed me along the path to the Old Siding. It was still difficult to know what to do, but I could at least get his model to come in through the gate instead of the house and through the paddock. The camera around Mr Antrobus's neck was bad enough, but if a young woman turned up the girls were sure to guess what was going on and I did not relish the subsequent conversation with their mother.

I was going to have to keep the girls in the paddock anyway, which wasn't going to be easy, and I could feel myself starting to panic as I showed Mr Antrobus the siding area and where the Strip led off to the north. He seemed dissatisfied, peering about as he had before and then taking his camera out and adjusting various settings. After a while he shook his head.

'No, I think the show jumps offer the most potential. Perhaps if the young ladies could be persuaded to use this space instead?'

He didn't sound very happy, not unreasonably as he'd booked the use of the land, and I resigned myself to trying to persuade Portia and Ophelia to ride up to the end of the strip, which also had the advantage of getting them out of the way. To my relief they agreed without even asking for an explanation, although as they left Ophelia made a joke to her sister, who laughed in return, then glanced at me and laughed again. Whatever Ophelia had said, I was sure of two things, that it was rude and that it involved me and Mr Antrobus, which had me pink with chagrin and once again wishing I could just take the little brat down across my knee and spank her until she howled, closely followed by her equally exasperating sister.

It was already gone seven, and Mr Antrobus was glancing impatiently at his watch as we came to the middle of the paddock. He tried ringing the model but her phone proved to be switched off and I began to wonder if she was going to turn up at all. He evidently thought the same, trying once more and then clicking his tongue in frustration when once again there was no answer.

'This will be the third no-show in a month!' he said after

a while.

'It's only been ten minutes,' I replied. 'Perhaps she's got her phone switched off because she's driving?'

'She's coming by train.'

'Oh. Well, never mind.'

I shrugged, trying to look sympathetic but secretly hoping the model wasn't going to come. In just under two hours I was supposed to be in my workshop, naked and with a saddle on my back, awaiting my lover. It was bad enough having Portia and Ophelia there, although I hoped they would leave in good time, but I could all too easily see Mr Antrobus outstaying his welcome. James would arrive and I'd still be dressed, which would ruin the moment I'd been slowly building up in my head ever since I'd got the letter.

Mr Antrobus had wandered off to have another peer over the hedges and managed to tread in horse dung, which he was trying to knock off by banging his shoe against the side of a jump. I walked across to him, glancing meaningfully at my watch as I came near.

'How long will you wait?'

'An hour,' he told. 'You understand that I won't be able to pay, of course?'

'Well, actually …'

'Unless,' he interrupted, 'one of your young friends might care to pose, or both?'

'The girls? No!'

'Why not? What young girl wouldn't like to go home with a twenty-pound note in her back pocket?'

'Those two. They're rather … you know, stuck up.'

'I will ask anyway,' he insisted, and favoured me with lewd wink, 'I expect you will be surprised.'

'No, really,' I assured him, horrified by the thought of him asking Portia and Ophelia to pose at all, never mind in the nude. 'Perhaps whatshername … Delilah will turn up after all?'

'I suspect not,' he said, peering at his watch, 'but I don't give up easily, not Paul Antrobus. The girls will do it, I'm sure, if I offer enough, unless of course you would be willing?'

'Me!?'

'Why not? I'm not one of these photographers who insists on every model he uses being under twenty-five, you know. In fact I appreciate the mature form and greater confidence of an older model. You're a little fleshy, perhaps, particularly around your bottom, but you have fine, big breasts and a good waist for your age. You'll do very nicely.'

I couldn't find an answer immediately, horrified by his suggestion and what he was saying, because while I was considerably older than Portia and Ophelia he had at least another twenty years on me and was an ugly little runt into the bargain. He carried on, perhaps mistaking my outrage for indecision.

'I have a great deal of experience, I assure you, and really it's only a question of finding the most flattering poses.'

I opened my mouth, thinking to suggest he try Portia and Ophelia after all, but I knew exactly what their reaction would be, a firm no followed by passing on the information to their mother, who was sure to blame me, and pass the gossip on to others. By the time it got round the village it would be as if I'd lured the girls on to my land and tried to make them strip for the entertainment of a dirty old man. If I did it and the girls saw me it would be almost as bad.

'Does it have to be nude?' I asked weakly.

'Yes,' he answered without hesitation. 'I am composing a study on the public reaction to nudity in unexpected situations, the idea being to challenge conventional preconceptions of what is and is not acceptable.'

I'd never heard such arrant tripe in my life, nor so flimsy an excuse to get women to strip, but I found myself nodding like an idiot. He went on.

'Perhaps actually the stable yard would be best? I had

thought to have Delilah89 putting up the show jumps, but I think I could create a stronger image if you were to have a bucket and shovel, to clean up the horse plop.'

'You want me to muck out in the nude?' I answered slowly.

'That's the expression is it, to muck out?' he answered. 'I must remember that. Yes, mucking out, nude. I actually think we might capture some very strong images here.'

Again I nodded, reflecting that at least if I was in the stable yard Portia and Ophelia weren't going to catch me, as while I was likely to hear them coming anyway, in the yard I definitely would and could make a dash for the shelter of the house. It was still an appalling prospect, and another problem had occurred to me.

'Hang on, are these pictures going to be published?'

'Oh no, they're strictly for my private collection.'

I wasn't sure I believed him, and if it was true it made an even bigger nonsense of his claim to want to challenge the preconceptions of whatever it was. Again I hesitated, wondering if I should simply throw him off my land, by main force if necessary. It would save me from having to muck out in the nude in front of him while he took photographs, but was sure to mean bad references on all the internet sites I'd used to advertise for photographers.

'It is art nude,' he said, 'nothing to be ashamed of, not femjoy or anything.'

'Femjoy?'

'Open leg shots, or taken from behind so that your anus shows.'

'Oh.'

I'd started to blush, thinking of how excited exactly that sort of pose made me in the right circumstances, especially when about to be spanked.

'Nothing to be ashamed of,' he repeated, 'but if you'd rather not, then that's up to you. I'll ask the girls.'

'No, really, don't,' I answered him, wondering if he was

55

spiteful enough to try and press an assault charge if I frogmarched him off my land. 'Just art nude, you say, while I muck out? OK.'

'Good girl,' he said, beaming, 'but we'd better hurry or we're going to lose the best of the evening light.'

I gave a mute nod and made for the house, trailing after him as he chattered about his project and the other girls he'd persuaded to strip nude in what sounded like highly personal and embarrassing situations, one on the platform of a country station with her suitcase but not a stitch of clothing, another naked in her car while they visited a supermarket, a third jogging on a lonely footpath. I seemed to be getting off lightly by comparison, but that was very little consolation as I stripped off my clothes in the workshop. He didn't even have the decency to turn his back, let alone go outside, his little dark eyes flickering over my body as I came bare, to drink in the quality of my breasts and hips, and bottom and thighs and belly, not openly lustful, but with a creepy fascination I found equally disturbing. When I was naked he nodded.

'Yes, you do have excellent breasts, full and heavy the way a mature woman's should be. Now, they're your best feature, so when you pose you need to be conscious of them all the time. Don't hunch up. Keep them pushed out, or let them loll so their roundness shows. Now turn around, let me see your bottom properly.'

I did as I was told, embarrassed and angry for the way he was describing my body, but also conscious of a strange desire to impress, perhaps because I knew he'd seen so many other women naked. As I turned I put my hands on my head and pulled my back in, sticking my bottom out a little to make the best of my curves. It was only then that I remembered that my cheeks were stripy with welts from my whipping, but it was too late, my bottom on full show, his gaze already drinking in my naked rear view and the implication of the long pink lines that crisscrossed my

56

cheeks. I could do nothing, and stood as I was, wishing my blush would go down at least a little bit and that I could stop my limbs from shaking. He seemed to take an age in his inspection, but finally spoke.

'Big, but nice and firm, just the way I imagine a stable girl. I see you do fetish?'

I knew what he meant from the websites, not that I was actually into kinky sex, but that I was willing to pose for fetishistic photographs. That in turn implied that I modelled regularly, but I didn't care any more. He'd given me an excuse, a way to explain my welts without admitting I liked to be beaten, and I actually felt grateful as I replied.

'Yes. I had a shoot last weekend.'

He laughed.

'Ah ha, now I see why you were a bit reluctant, but don't mind me. I've seen it all, believe you me. It is a bit of a shame though, because of course you wouldn't expect a stable girl to have been whipped, not normally.'

'You might if …,' I began, and stopped, deciding against explaining that a girl made to muck out in the nude was probably being punished, in which case she might well have been whipped beforehand. The scenario was far too close to my fantasies.

'I can always take the marks out in processing,' he said, more to himself than to me. 'Right then, in your wellies, I think, and a bucket and spade?'

'Shovel,' I corrected him automatically, and went to get one.

I felt even more exposed in just my wellies than I had stark naked. It seemed to add a smutty touch, robbing me of whatever artistic value there might have been in my nudity and leaving me simply as an object of male fantasy. As we came back outside I was still hoping that the real model might turn up, but Mr Antrobus seemed to have forgotten all about her, with his face set in a frown of concentration as he adjusted the settings on his camera and took test shots of

57

pieces of brick wall. I was left standing in the nude, listening out for Portia and Ophelia, although to my immense relief there was no sign of them either. Finally Mr Antrobus looked up.

'Let us begin. We'll need some horse plop first.'

He was right. With no horse of my own the yard was fairly clean, while I'd been shovelling the mess left by the girls' horses onto a manure heap in a corner of the paddock. I found myself a wheelbarrow and went to get some, but Mr Antrobus immediately asked me to stop and took a picture of me pushing the wheelbarrow under the arch, from an angle clearly designed to emphasise my bottom before moving around to one side.

'Remember, let your breasts loll forward,' he instructed.

'I didn't realise we'd started,' I protested, but I'd done as I was told, leaning forward a little to show off the curve of my back and the size of my boobs.

'Good girl,' he said, not bothering to answer my question. 'Now into the paddock.'

I went, quickly, sure that Portia and Ophelia would turn up at any moment, but Mr Antrobus seemed determined to capture every possibility offered by the sight of me shovelling manure in the nude. He'd taken at least a couple of dozen pictures before my wheelbarrow was full, while I'd been put in every pose I could have imagined at least twice and some distinctly peculiar ones as well. Most of them involved sticking out my bottom, and despite his promises I was sure some of the pictures would show my fanny from behind and very probably my bumhole too.

Three times he made me fill the wheelbarrow and empty it out into the yard, until the corner where the wall joined my workshop was filled with manure and fresh dung. It was steaming, long white tendrils rising in the cool evening sunlight, a shot he was particularly keen to capture, so that I was obliged first to stand beside the pile with my hand on my hip as if proud of what I'd done, then to pretend to shovel it with my bottom thrust out to the camera and my breasts lolling forward the way he liked it. By then I was sweaty and less than clean, with mud on my knees and streaks from the manure on my legs where I'd accidentally brushed against the wheelbarrow.

'Nearly done,' he said cheerfully, 'but if you could, perhaps, just smear a little on your breasts?'

'What!?'

'Smear a little manure on your breasts, please, not too much or it will look contrived.'

'How about my face too while we're at it?' I demanded, my voice dripping sarcasm.

'Hum ... yes, you're right,' he answered, apparently oblivious, 'but just a little, don't over do it.'

'Look I ... oh for goodness' sake!'

I was filthy anyway, and feeling utterly humiliated, for what I'd done, but far, far more for the fact that it was starting to get to me, being nude in front of him and being photographed in the nude. Dirty tits and a little mess on my face wasn't going to make much difference. My hands were already dirty, and I wiped my forehead and one cheek to streak myself with filth, then dug my hands into the pile to pull out two good handfuls of manure, which I slapped onto my breasts, holding it there for an instant before shaking it off.

'OK?' I demanded. Is that what you wanted?'

'A little over the top, perhaps,' he said, 'but yes, if you turn sideways, now bend down so they loll right forward ... yes, like that. Now stick the shovel well in, low down ... yes, and your right leg out to brace yourself ... and hold your pose ... now feet together, bottom up ...'

I obeyed, for all that I knew what I was showing, because it was more or less the same pose James had made me adopt to show off my fanny and bottom hole to humiliate me while I was whipped. The camera clicked, then again, both side views, then again, right behind me from a position that couldn't fail to have captured every rude detail of my rear view.,

'And that's a naughty one just for me,' he chuckled. 'Thank you, Amber, that was very good of you, and it's just gone eight-thirty, so I'll pay you an hour and a half.'

'Eight-thirty?' I demanded.

'Eight-thirty-seven to be precise,' he said, frowning over his camera. 'Would you like to see the images?'

'No, thank you. Actually I'm in a bit of a hurry. I have an appointment at nine.'

He merely nodded and carried on with his inspection of the pictures in the back of the camera. I'd had no idea it was so late, leaving me with just twenty minutes to get rid of him, wash and get myself ready for James. Not that I needed any more preparation when it came to being ready to submit myself sexually. What Mr Antrobus had done to me had left me shaking with reaction and so full of chagrin that had he been even marginally more appealing I'd have offered to suck him off and done myself while I knelt on the filthy ground with his cock in my mouth. Not that I had the time anyway, nor to worry about my modesty when it came to washing, especially as he'd seen everything anyway.

I went to the tap, kicked my boots off and turned it full on, grabbing the hose and directing it straight at my filthy tits. He began to take photographs again, but I was past caring, rubbing urgently at my dirty skin as the cold water cascaded down my body without thought for what I was showing, even when it came to washing my fanny and between my cheeks. He never said a word, but he was smiling by the time I'd finished and made some remark about giving me a little bonus.

His words barely penetrated, and I took the slim sheaf of notes he was holding out to me as I made for the kitchen door. They were five pounds notes, twenty in all, in two lots of ten, fifty pounds for the use of my land, and fifty pounds for the use of my body, the price of having me shovel shit in the nude for an hour and a half. Only as I saw the pile of grubby little notes lying there on the kitchen table did it really sink in that I had sold myself, one of those things that really gets to me, which I hate, and yet which brings me to a state of excitement beyond my ability to control.

If Mr Antrobus had pulled out his cock at that moment and demanded that I suck it I'd have been straight down on my knees, and quicker still if he'd offered to pay. As it was he simply left, as oblivious to my feelings as he had been since his arrival, not even trying to kiss me goodbye. In fact he hadn't touched me at all, even to make me pose the way he wanted, but he'd got me in a desperate state, so turned on I could hardly keep my hands off my body and completely off balance, just right for James, maybe, but too much for me to be waiting on all fours with my saddle on my back.

I went out to the workshop anyway, relieved to have got rid of Mr Antrobus, although it had been close, with just five minutes to spare. Portia and Ophelia were another matter, but it was starting to get dark, so they'd presumably gone home. I was in no state to check, still naked and shaking with arousal, and it seemed sensible to have James ensure that the coast was clear once he'd found me in the position he'd ordered. With the workshop door shut I was safe anyway, as I'd surely hear them in plenty of time, but as I hurried to pull on my harness I was shaking so badly I could barely do up the straps.

With the saddle on my back I felt ruder still, now ready to be ridden about the room on all fours, showing everything from behind, perhaps even with a tail up my bottom, certainly in a head harness and bit. I needed knee pads too, and quickly pulled them on, then my bridle, but it was just too much. There was only one way to calm myself down, and if James caught me at it so much the better. He'd punish me, and if my bottom wasn't ready for another whipping then there were other ways to teach a girl a lesson.

I got down on all fours the way he'd ordered me to and

closed my eyes, forcing myself to take deep, even breaths as I let my fingers slip between my thighs, but I needed attention to my breasts too and quickly put my face and chest to the ground, rubbing them in the sawdust on the floor and stroking them too as I began to masturbate. Mr Antrobus was right, they are big, and heavy, so I thought of how he'd made me pose, again and again in positions that left me with my boobs lolling forward, just the way they do when I bend for the whip or cane, or when I go on all fours to have my bottom spanked, or lick another woman, or suck cock, or even take a man from behind, crawling on all fours like a dog as some bastard feeds his fat, pink erection up my cunt or worse, forces my bottom hole.

As my pleasure rose I was wishing Mr Antrobus had made me go on all fours, crawling in the mud with my boobs dangling down, even in the heap of manure with my bottom lifted as he photographed me deliberately degrading myself. I wondered if he'd have been able to resist sticking his cock up my obviously willing hole and fucking me as I knelt in the filthy mess, but the thought of his whiny voice telling me to stick my bottom up and his clammy little hands taking hold of my hips as he pushed his erection in was more than I could bear. I wanted James, with his cool, assertive manner and exact understanding of the way I would react. He could have me on all fours any time he wanted, and in a few minutes he was going to do just that.

I cried out, wishing James was already there with his lovely pale cock jammed deep up my bottom and his balls squashed to my empty cunt as he buggered me. He'd ride me for a while, with a pony-tail stuck up my bottom to show me off and get me greasy, enjoying his control over me and my abject submission. Only when he was good and ready would he dismount, to stick his cock in my mouth while he played with the tail in my bumhole, feeding the plug in and out until I was juicy and ready.

When he was hard he would go around behind me, pull

out the tail and order me to take it in my mouth, sucking on the plug that had just been up my bottom as he rubbed his cock between my fanny lips. He'd fuck me, briefly, just to let me know he'd been up my cunt, then push his lovely big erection slowly in up my straining bottom hole, holding on to my saddle as he buggered me. That thought was enough, and I cried out again as I started to come, in blinding ecstasy, even as I heard the click of the door catch and I knew he was with me, watching me masturbate shamelessly over what we would shortly be doing.

'You dirty bitch!'

The words were right, but not the voice, no commanding male drawl but a distinctly female squeal of shock, but also of unmistakable delight, and my eyes came open to look up into the face not of James Sebastian, but of Portia and Ophelia Crowthorne-Jones.

Chapter Five

My first thought was that I'd managed to embarrass myself again, and in a worse fashion than the first time, at least until Portia tried to climb on my back. I couldn't cope with that at all and I got to my feet, easily resisting her attempt to push me back down on to all fours. What followed was more a blur of noise than a conversation, with all three of us trying to speak at the same time, but I finally managed to assert myself.

'We need to talk,' I told them, and both nodded.

By then Ophelia was close to tears, but her sister was made of sterner stuff, simply leaning back against the door, presumably to prevent me from escaping, and watching while I pulled off my harness and wrapped myself in an old towel. Even in the initial confusion I'd managed to ascertain that they'd sent the letter, not James, who was presumably at his flat and blissfully unaware of what was going on, or at least I earnestly hoped he was, and of course there was no reason to suppose that they knew anything about him and me. While that was going to mean a bit of explaining, I was determined to keep it that way.

'So you want to play with me?' I demanded, doing my best to exert my authority as the older woman despite the way they'd just seen me.

'Yes,' Portia admitted, her voice full of exasperation. 'So what's the problem? If you didn't want us, what were you doing like that?'

'I ... I didn't realise the letter was from you!' I blurted

out, only to realise that I was digging a hole for myself. 'I thought … I thought it was from my partner.'

'Your girlfriend, Kay?'

'Yes, of course, but … but how do you know all this? Who told you I like to be a pony-girl, for goodness sake!?

'Everybody in the village knows you're a lesbian,' Ophelia put in, using the same defensive tone she'd employed from the start.

'Being a lesbian is one thing,' I answered her. 'Enjoying being put in harness is quite another, and besides, what makes you think … oh, never mind, let's just say I prefer to be the rider.'

'You could have fooled me!' Portia laughed.

I had to admire her sheer arrogance, and even Ophelia was doing her best to tough it out, but I wanted the truth.

'Tell me how you knew?' I demanded.

'Why should we?' Portia answered.

'Not if you won't play with us,' Ophelia added.

'I didn't say I wouldn't play with you,' I told them, 'but you could just have asked, couldn't you?'

'I thought,' Portia began, 'you know, that you'd like to be ordered to do it … I mean, you do, don't you, or you wouldn't have done as you were told, even for Kay, would you?'

For the first time she sounded unsure of herself, and I hastened to answer.

'Kay's my girlfriend. You should have said something first.'

'So you'll play?' Ophelia asked.

'Not if you're not going to tell me how you know I like that sort of thing,' I countered.

They looked at each other. Ophelia made a funny face. Portia nodded, then spoke.

'OK, I'll tell you. Gemma and I found out.'

'Who's Gemma?' I demanded, although I had a nasty suspicion that I already knew.

'She has bright red hair and big glasses,' Ophelia informed me, confirming my worst fears. 'I think you might have seen her at the gymkhana in Bayden.'

'And we know you saw her near the traveller's caravans along Cutler's Lane,' Portia added, confident once more, 'don't we? Because she saw you, and so did I, Amber, after you'd been spanked by those travellers and when you where in your car, playing with your dirty little cunt.'

Her voice was thick with relish as she spoke the last three words, evidently enjoying my discomfort immensely, as was her now giggling sister.

'So that was you?' I asked, and I'd given up all pretence of denying what I'd done.

'Yes,' she said, 'so come on, we know what you're like, Amber.'

'We told you, so now you have to play,' Ophelia added. 'Doesn't she, Portia?'

'Yes,' Portia repeated. 'Come on, Miss Oakley, we want our fun.'

It was only then that I realised they were both slightly drunk. Something wasn't quite right either, because while they might have figured out that I liked to be spanked, rather than assuming I'd been punished, and obviously realised that I was highly sexed, there was no way they could know about my liking for pony-girl play. Unfortunately it was obvious, although it had to have taken a lot of nerve, even for an arrogant little brat like Portia.

Once I'd gone they'd have gone to the caravan. Hannah and Maggie knew, just about everything, only it wouldn't have been Hannah they'd spoken to. Hannah would have sent them away with fleas in their ears, if not smacked bottoms, but not Maggie. Maggie would have told them, just to humiliate me, and she had succeeded. It made sense, but she couldn't have known what Portia's reaction would be, so it was actually quite funny. Instead of making me a public disgrace she'd managed to find me two beautiful new

66

playmates, except of course that they wanted to do to me exactly what I wanted to do to them. Still, sometimes you have to give a little to get what you want, and more often than not it's the older, more experience person who has to give way to make it happen.

'OK,' I said with a sigh, 'what would you little perverts like to do first?'

'I want you back in that saddle,' Portia answered, her eyes bright with lust and cruelty, 'but maybe a punishment first?'

'Make her pee in her panties!' Ophelia suggested.

'She hasn't got any on,' Portia pointed out.

'Let's do it all over her then, and make her drink it!'

Portia merely smiled and gave her sister a friendly cuff around the head.

'Oh come on,' Ophelia urged, 'please? I'd love to do it in her mouth, and all over her hair, and I want to spank her too.'

'Blame the internet,' Portia said in response to my look of astonishment. It might be Portia who was in charge, and the crueller of the two, but Ophelia was the really dirty one.

'She deserves a spanking at the very least,' Ophelia insisted.

'Why?' I demanded.

'For being so stuck-up,' she answered me, 'oh so prim and proper, and all the time we've known what you're like!'

'Me stuck-up?' I demanded. 'You're the ones …'

'Will you two shut up and let me think,' Portia insisted. 'You look like you've already had a whipping, Amber? Show us your bottom again.'

I turned, reluctantly, to lift my towel and show them the welts on my cheeks.

'How did you get those marks?' Portia asked.

'From Hannah,' I lied.

'The big traveller woman?' Ophelia asked. 'She whips you as well as spanks you?'

I nodded. The way they were treating me was beginning to draw my thoughts back towards submissive sex, especially with Portia inspecting my whipped bottom. Her fingers found my skin, a gentle touch, very feminine, which sent a shock of excitement through me and before I really knew what I was doing I'd stuck my bottom out.

'Bend right down,' she demanded. 'I want to see it all.'

They came closer as I bent myself across my workbench, my eyes shut in deep shame but a great deal of pleasure as well. So often I'd fantasised over them and now they were inspecting my rear view, nude, their delicate fingers tracing out the lines of my welts where I'd been beaten, pinching and squeezing my flesh, slapping my cheeks to make them bounce, a sight that made Ophelia giggle and draw a sob from my mouth.

'You have a huge bottom,' Portia remarked, 'just right for spanking, or whipping.'

'Or peeing on,' Ophelia added, 'that's what I want to do, Portia, pee all over her big fat bottom.'

'Shut up,' Portia told her, 'or I'll do it on you. Hmm … yes, you could take a little more, I think. OK, stand up, get rid of that towel and put your hands on your head.'

I obeyed, letting my towel drop to the floor to go naked once more. They stood back, their eyes lingering on my body, Portia cruel and calculating, Ophelia eager and excited. At last Portia nodded.

'And now, Miss Oakley,' Portia said, 'we are going to spank you.'

'Over our knees,' Ophelia added, 'on your bare bottom.'

'I think she knows how a spanking should be delivered,' Portia went on. 'In fact, I'm sure she knows. Don't you, Miss Oakley?'

I couldn't answer, dumbstruck for what they intended to do to me, and for what they obviously knew, but for all my horror I found myself nodding weakly. Portia had sat down, and now patted her lap in the all-too-familiar signal, but

Ophelia was less confident in my compliance and had taken me firmly by one arm. She needn't have bothered, because my will to resist had dissolved completely as I allowed myself to be drawn down across her sister's knee and into spanking position.

It wasn't the first time I'd been over a younger woman's knee, but it always gets to me, while Portia was a lot younger. Yet what she lacked in age she made up for in natural dominance, and she obviously knew what she was doing, taking my arm and twisting it up into the small of my back to hold me in place, then twisting one of her legs around one of mine to pull my thighs open and spread my cunt to her sister's delighted gaze.

'That's lovely,' Ophelia breathed. 'Go on, Portia, spank her, spank her hard!'

'Bum up, Amber,' Portia ordered, ignoring her sister, 'let's see between those big cheeks.'

I hesitated and she slapped me, my first slap from her, but I knew it wouldn't be my last, not by a long way.

'Bum up!' she repeated.

This time I did as I was told, lifting my bottom to let my cheeks part and show off my anus.

'What a rude bottom hole she has!' Ophelia giggled. 'Oh you ought to see yourself, Amber, with your big fat bum in the air. I'm going to enjoy you!'

'Keep it like that,' Portia ordered. 'Now then, you stuck-up bitch!'

She began to spank me, as hard as she could with my arm still twisted hard into the small of my back, so that I was gasping with pain and kicking my legs, making an even ruder show of my rear view than before. Ophelia began to laugh, and to talk again, driving my humiliation ever higher as Portia spanked me.

'Oh, just look at her! What a sight! Look at it all bounce, Portia, and way her bottom hole winks! Let me have a go.'

Portia transferred her attention to just one of my cheeks

and Ophelia set to work on the other, spanking to an even rhythm and laughing at me as I kicked and jerked to the smacks. It hurt like anything, but even if it hadn't, just being across Portia's knee would have been too much for me, never mind Ophelia's open delight in my pain and the rude display of my bottom. I burst into tears, blubbering out my feelings across my persecutor's lap as the two of them spanked me and my head burned with the appalling humiliation of being punished nude by two young girls, girls I'd wanted to give the same treatment so badly and now I was lying across one's knee, stark naked with my bottom bouncing to their slaps. They didn't stop, enjoying themselves too much to care that I was in tears, or perhaps aware that I usually cry when I'm spanked.

'What a cry baby!' Ophelia crowed, and I was sure that it was Maggie who'd told her.

Maggie always enjoyed my tears, and liked to taunt me because I cried. I was swearing revenge as my spanking continued, for all that my cheeks were now hot and my head buzzing with arousal. The girls didn't seem to care either way, just enjoying my bum without thought for my response, until at last Ophelia stopped.

'Ow! My hand stings. I know, I'm going to put something up her.'

'Hey, no ...' I began, but broke off with a yelp of pain as Portia twisted my arm tighter still and at the same instant slapped me hard across the back of my thighs.

'You do as you're told,' she ordered. 'Now stay still. What are you doing, sis? Oh my, it's one of her tails! Yes, put that in her.'

'No, look, girls,' I blustered as I twisted around to find Ophelia with one of my cupboards open and a plug-in pony-girl tail in her hand. 'Seriously, you need to be careful ... ow!'

'Shut up!' Portia snapped, applying another volley of smacks to the back of my thighs. 'We know what to do. The

70

plug goes up your bottom hole, doesn't it?'

'Yes,' I admitted, 'but you need plenty of lubricant.'

'We know,' she said and she slid a hand between my cheeks to spread my anus.

Ophelia giggled at the sight, then turned her attention back to the cupboard, pulling out a big tube of anal lubricant. I hung my head, resigned to my fate as Portia began to tease my anus, tickling the little hole to make it wink and set her sister laughing again. A moment later I felt a cool, slimy sensation as a thick worm of lubricant was laid across my stretched-out hole, then Portia's finger once more, burrowing into my ring.

I couldn't hold back a sigh as I was penetrated, and I'd already stuck my bottom higher still to make it easier for them, and less painful for me. Yet my helpless excitement only went so far to soothe my feelings, and I was unable to keep the sulky expression off my face as Portia opened my bottom hole up. She'd put her finger right in and was wiggling it about while her evil little sister smeared lubricant onto the plug that was about to go up me. A second finger went up my bottom, to make me gasp and then set me sobbing in raw shame as she spread them to stretch my anus open for the insertion of the plug.

'Stick it in,' Portia instructed and she'd pulled out her fingers to leave my anus a gaping hole between my spread bottom cheeks.

'Make her suck your fingers,' Ophelia giggled even as she pressed the tip of the tail plug to my anus.

'You're a disgrace, Ophelia,' Portia answered, but her hand had come down to the level of my face, offering the two fingers she'd just had up my bottom to my mouth. 'You heard, Amber, suck them.'

I just couldn't stop myself. My mouth came wide, in went her fingers and my mouth filled with the taste of lubricant and my own bottom as I began to suck. Ophelia gave a squeal of mingled disgust and delight as she saw that

71

I'd obeyed her filthy command, then began to push the tail plug in up my bottom. Portia pulled her fingers free and I forced myself to relax, grimacing as my ring spread to the pressure of the plug. I knew I could take it though, because it was hardly the first time, for all that I'd never before had one inserted by two vicious little bitches who wouldn't stop laughing at the sight of my spread, spanked bottom and my straining hole.

Soon the plug was in and I felt my ring close on the shaft. It was my favourite tail, with a slim extension to the shaft running up between my cheeks so that it appeared to protrude from the base of my spine s if it were real, and a hank of curly golden hair to match my own. With the tail fully in Portia finally let go of my wrist and I was allowed to stand up, now with the tail rising above my pink bottom.

'Now the saddle and harness,' Portia ordered. 'We're going to ride you, and if you're very good, maybe we'll let you lick our pussies. Would you like that?'

I nodded, unable to deny the truth. Just the way she was sitting was a temptation, with her legs spread and the material of her jodhpurs taut over her sex to show off the outline of her lips and the slit between. She was wet, and she wasn't the only one, the juice from my fanny now warm and slippery between my thighs as it began to trickle down. Portia could see, and her face was set in cruel amusement for my reaction as she sat back to watch me put my harness back on, cool and calm for all her own arousal. Ophelia was less reticent, watching wide-eyed and with her mouth a little open, one hand gently stroking the mound of her fanny through the front of her jodhpurs.

It seemed to take for ever to get my harness on properly, especially the bridle, and with each strap fastened my feelings grew a little stronger until by the time I was ready I could even find it in me to feel resentment for what they'd done. I got down, on to all fours, waiting to be mounted every bit as meekly as I'd done when I'd thought it would be

72

James Sebastian riding me. Portia stood up, to walk slowly over to me, picking up her riding crop from my workbench as she came.

'Pretty horsie,' she said, and tapped the end of her crop against my bottom. 'Stay still, there's a good girl.'

She swung a leg over me and I felt her weight settle on my back. Another tap to my bottom and I'd begun to crawl. My tears began to run again, just for the way I was, crawling along the floor of my own workshop, harnessed and saddled like a beast of burden, my bottom pink from spanking, my anus stretched to the plug of a pony-girl tail with the hank of hair swinging from side to side across my cheeks as I moved, and with Portia riding on my back. She realised I was crying and responded with an odd little clicking noise in her throat, maybe excitement, maybe pure cruelty.

Again she smacked her crop against my flesh, on my hip this time and as she tugged on my reins to make me turn, only not towards her sister as I'd expected, but at the door. I hesitated, caught another, harder smack for my pains and I was responding even as the giggling Ophelia ran to pull the door wide. It was dark outside, the yard illuminated only by the light from my kitchen windows. I knew I was safe, but that didn't stop me feeling intensely vulnerable as Portia steered me towards the yet darker gap of the arch with Ophelia walking beside us.

They took me out into the paddock, where they took turns with me, one after the other riding me up and down, often laughing, often applying their crops to my bottom and thighs, sometimes pausing to feel my breasts or fanny, using me exactly as they pleased until I was aching and sore but too high on my own submission to do anything about it, or want to. By the time they eventually tired of the game I was exhausted. I'd lost all track of time and I was dizzy with arousal, but I knew they still had more in store for me.

'You make a very good horse,' Portia told me as she finally climbed off my back, now in my workshop once more. 'I'd give you a peppermint if I had any, but we fed them all to the real horses, speaking of which, we're going to have to start back soon, sis, so we'd better get on with it.'

'I want to come,' Ophelia sighed.

'So do I,' Portia agreed. 'Right, strip off, Amber, but take your tail out last.'

I began to undo the buckles, pulling off the heavy saddle first, then my bridle. My skin was slick with sweat and sore in places, while I hadn't really been ready for spanking, and my welts stung, especially where they'd used the crop on me.

'May I leave my knee pads on please, Miss Portia?' I asked, and was rewarded with a little smile for addressing her politely.

'Yes,' she answered. 'Now take your tail out.'

I reached back, to take hold of the pony-girl tail and ease the plug gently out of my bottom hole.

'In your mouth,' Portia ordered, her voice now hoarse 'Suck on it.'

Ophelia gave a moan of pleasure as I obeyed, taking the fat, black butt plug in my mouth and sucking on it as my anus closed. I saw Portia swallow and she had spread her thighs, showing the crotch of her jodhpurs, now soaking with her juice. She beckoned to me, but her sister interrupted.

'Me first, please, I can't wait.'

She was already pushing down her jodhpurs, baring her slender hips and long, smooth thighs, also showing off a pair of tight white panties that hugged the contours of her body and clung tight to the outline of her sex, which was as wet as her sister's. It was my turn to swallow as I imagined being allowed to lick such a pretty fanny, and again as she pushed down her panties to show off her bare mound, her lips puffy with excitement and her slit glistening with moisture.

'Would you like to lick my sister's pussy?' Portia asked

I nodded urgently, then pulled the plug out of my mouth

and Ophelia came close, pushing out her hips to show off her sex. My tongue came out and I'd buried my face in her fanny, lapping up her juices and wriggling my lips and nose against her flesh. At last I had contact with her, and if it wasn't in the way I might have wished it was no less wonderful for that. I'd soon be doing Portia as well, a yet more delicious prospect, and as I busied myself with Ophelia's cunt I'd slipped a hand back between my thighs. As I began to masturbate I was half expecting Portia to order me to stop, but she seemed content to enjoy the view, and perhaps the state they'd got me in.

'That's lovely,' Ophelia sighed. 'Let me sit down.'

Portia was on the only nearby chair, and Ophelia sat down in her sister's lap, pushing her jodhpurs and panties down to the level of her boots as she did so. She spread her thighs, offering me her little pink cunt once more as Portia took hold of her around the waist to keep her steady. I crawled across and began to lick again, and to rub at myself as Ophelia fumbled open the buttons of her blouse to expose two small, braless breasts topped by hard pink nipples. She began to play with them, only for Portia to move her hands higher, cupping her own sister's breasts as I continued to lick.

Ophelia gave a long sigh and her hands had found my hair, tangling in among my curls to pull my head closer in. Her thighs were high and wide, her sweetly turned cheeks a little open, exposing the puckered, dun coloured mouth of her anus. I couldn't resist, and kissed the little tight ring, then began to lick.

'She's licking my bottom,' Ophelia sighed. 'Oh, yes please, like that, Amber … lick my bottom hole.'

I didn't need telling, my tongue flicking over the bumps and crevices of her neat brown star as I masturbated. My pleasure was rising fast as I did it, quickly getting ruder, with my tongue tip pushed in up her slippery bumhole as I worked my cunt. She'd begun to make little purring noises and had her legs cocked wide as far as they would go, spreading her fanny in my face and her bottom to my mouth. I stuck my tongue deeper, right into the muscular little ring of her anus, tasting her as I started to come.

My head was full of what they'd done to me, the way they'd spanked me and made me go in harness, having my own anus opened and the pony-girl tail stuck in, being made to suck Portia's fingers when they'd been up my bottom, all the little indignities and humiliations they'd subjected me to while they rode me, and before, treating me like dirt, and all of it coming together in one perfect moment as I reached orgasm with my tongue stuck as deep as it would go up Ophelia Crowthorne-Jones's bottom hole.

They knew I was coming and Portia was laughing at me, but Ophelia was too far gone to find it amusing, even with me masturbating to orgasm over the pleasure of licking her anus. She wanted her cunt licked and was trying to pull my head up higher, but I held off despite the pain, taking my full dose of ecstasy before giving in and transferring the attentions of my tongue to her clitoris. From the moment I touched the little bud she was gasping, and babbling too, ordering me to do it harder and calling me a bitch, begging her sister to squeeze her tits and twisting her fist in my hair.

Her words broke to a cry of ecstasy and she was there, her legs locking tight around my head and her fingers jerking at my hair as she pulled me hard against her cunt, her back arched as she thrust herself into my face. I did my best to please, licking hard for all the pain and that my face was so firmly smothered into her sex that I could barely breathe. When at last she let go I pulled quickly back, gasping for breath as she went slowly limp in her sister's arms, and it was just as well that Portia was holding her or she'd have ended up on the floor.

My tongue was sore, my fanny too, my face smeared with Ophelia's juices and my mouth full of the taste of her body, but I still wasn't done. Portia hadn't come, and I could see that she was in no mood to let me off. Her eyes were glittering with cruelty and pleasure as she sent her sister on her way with a well judged slap to one tight bottom cheek and we were left face to face, she seated spread-legged on the chair, fully dressed but with the crotch of her jodhpurs sodden with her juices, me kneeling nude on the floor, filthy with dirt and sweat, my face soiled with her sister's juices, my rosy bottom pushed well out and my boobs lolling before me.

'I knew you were dirty,' she said, her voice oddly deep and thick with arousal, 'but to lick another woman's bottom? That's ... that's lovely. Come on, Amber, lick mine too. Would you like to lick my bottom? I bet you would ... come on, please?'

She'd broken suddenly, abandoning her poise to reveal herself for the filthy little slut she was at heart, by word, and by deed. Even as she'd spoken she'd twisted round, to kneel on the chair with her bottom pushed well out into a split ball of taut girlflesh, filling out her jodhpurs to perfection. I crawled close, more than happy to lick her from behind, and to put my tongue just as deep up her bumhole as it would go.

'Do it,' she ordered, once more trying to sound firm, 'pull down my jodhpurs and stick your tongue in where it belongs, right up my bottom hole. No, kiss it first ... kiss my bottom hole, Amber, then get your tongue in.'

My hands were already on the waistband of her jodhpurs, but unlike her I'd just come and took my time over the moment, peeling them slowly down over her perfect little bottom. She had no panties on, and came bare in my face, first the beautiful roundness of her cheeks, then the slit between and the puckered little star I had to kiss, darker than her sister's, but every bit as sweetly formed. Her fanny came bare as I tugged the jodhpurs lower still, equally lovely, the twin lips pouting from between her thighs, a cunt as perfect as her bottom, and slippery with juice.

'Go on,' Ophelia demanded. 'Kiss her bottom hole,

Amber, and let me see.'

I obliged, spreading Portia's bottom open with my hands to show off her anus as I puckered up. Ophelia gave a pleased sigh and Portia an impatient wriggle, but I wanted to savour the moment, admiring the tight brown ring in front of my face for a few seconds to let what I was about to do sink in, to kiss another woman's bottom hole, to willingly press my lips to a girl's anus, and not just any girl, Portia Crowthorne-Jones.

'Kiss my hole, you piece of dirt!' Portia snapped, and I'd done it.

My lips touched her anus, a gentle, submissive kiss, to thank her for what she'd done to me and to let her know who was boss. It was the perfect gesture, my lips pressed to her bumhole, leaving no doubt who was in charge, who was the Mistress and who was the grovelling little slut, a piece of dirt as she'd called me, and with that my hands had gone back to my cunt and breasts. Ophelia laughed to see me masturbating again, but I'd stuck my tongue up Portia's bumhole and her response was a happy sigh.

'As deep as you can,' she demanded, 'and get your hands off your fat boobies and on to my pussy, you greedy bitch.'

I complied, putting a knuckle to her clit as I tried to force my tongue deeper still into her anus. My other hand was still busy with my cunt though and I could already feel the first twinges of another orgasm coming on. Again Portia moaned and I began to rub harder, bumping my finger over the tiny bud between her sex lips as I licked at her bottom, her pussy, and her bottom once more, smothering my face between her lovely little cheeks as I pushed my tongue back up her hole.

Her moans grew louder, she cried out in wordless ecstasy and she was coming, full against my face with her anus squeezing on my tongue as her contractions began. I was on the edge myself, rubbing my own cunt as urgently as I was rubbing hers, with a myriad filthy thoughts running through my head, everything that they'd done to me, but best of all that final, awful detail, being made to kiss her anus. She'd come, her muscles growing slack as she slumped down, but I stayed as I was, my tongue still well up her bottom until my own orgasm had run its course and pulling back only when I was satisfied.

'Bad girls,' Ophelia sighed. 'That was lovely.'

I nodded, now in a state of bliss for all my aching, soiled body, and even Portia sounded happy when she finally found her voice.

'It was, and you are going to be our pet, aren't you, Amber?'

I nodded.

Chapter Six

I might have become their pet, but that didn't mean I had to be happy about the way it had come about. Ophelia was sweet, for all her airs and graces, a natural sadist and yet delightfully innocent, suggesting the filthiest things without a flicker of guilt. Even Portia I could forgive, for all that she was an authentic little bitch, because she was young and had obviously been reading too many BDSM novels for her own good. Both were also beautiful, and while I knew full well that shouldn't have made any difference, it did.

The one person I couldn't forgive was Maggie. The girls hadn't actually admitted it as such, but from what they knew it was obvious that she'd not only told them I like to be spanked, but just about every other detail of my sex life, going back years. The fact that my arrangement was with Hannah made no difference, or that it was Hannah who'd promised to keep my desires private. Maggie was her friend and confidant, and also took full advantage of me when she was there, often spanking me and almost always having me lick her out. I'd been good, putting up with her inverted snobbery and indulging her dirty habits, so I had every right to feel betrayed.

What to do about it was another matter. If I confronted her she could simply deny it, and I had no proof at all, unless I could persuade Portia or Ophelia to come clean, and they'd been extremely evasive when asked. More likely, she'd just laugh at me, or put me over her knee and spank me pink, while still laughing at me. Possibly I could complain to Hannah, but they'd known each other since they were children and stuck together like glue. Again, it was a very good way to end up getting a spanking, but otherwise not much use. Eventually I decided I'd just have to put up with it, save that the next time I visited I would make sure that Hannah was alone.

Not that I really needed to visit, with Portia and Ophelia to attend to me and my budding affair with James Sebastian into the bargain. Yet there was something about the way Hannah spanked me that nobody else I knew could deliver, certainly not Portia and Ophelia, either of who I could have taken across my knee and dealt with soundly without breaking a sweat. I might even have done exactly that, had I felt they'd have been able to cope with punishment even half as well as they dished it out.

They certainly deserved it, despite the ecstasy they'd given me, because for all my mixed feelings, if there's one thing I can't abide it's somebody who loves to dish it out but is too stuck-up to take it in her turn. With men I didn't mind so much, perhaps illogically, but then I've never taken more than a detached pleasure in physically punishing men, cruel but asexual. Hannah I just put up with, as if she were some elemental force, and besides, I knew she'd been spanked in her time and the fact that she was now too strong and massive for anybody to do it was one of the things which added to my own pleasure when she was dishing it out to me. Other women were another matter, and if two girls had ever deserved to have their bottoms roasted it was Portia and Ophelia Crowthorne-Jones.

I fully intended to have them both, but in the fullness of time. For the moment that meant being their pet, meek and obedient, more or less regardless of what they asked. That was going to mean plenty of spankings, maybe harder punishments, pony-girl play and no doubt other kinky amusements.

By the time we'd finished and cleaned up they'd been in

a hurry to get home, so they'd retrieved their horses from the Old Siding and left without much in the way of conversation. I'd gone indoors, so tired that I fell asleep in my badly needed bath and woke up to chilly water and aching muscles at some point in the early hours of the morning. By the time I woke up again it was gone nine and Marjorie Crowthorne-Jones was out in the paddock. I couldn't help but smile at the thought of what I'd been up to with her daughters, and settled down to breakfast sore but happy, save only for my niggling irritation with Maggie.

I was still sipping at my coffee when James called, asking me if I'd like to come to lunch at the Golden Lion the next day. Only when I'd accepted did I realise that seeing him would almost certainly mean my knickers coming down, which meant having to explained the extra marks left by Portia and Ophelia's riding crops, if there were any. I was only in an old top over panties, so it was easy to bare my bottom for a quick inspection in the bathroom mirror, which showed that I'd probably get away with it. There were only a few faint marks in addition to the welts from his switch, and those were fading. Another day would not only be safe but leave me ready for more.

Just going bare like that had me smiling and thinking naughty thoughts of what I might get from James, and with the girls. It was an exciting prospect, although not without a touch of chagrin for the fact that I would be the one getting it on both occasions. Again I started to consider my wicked plan for turning the tables on the girls, wondering if there was some clever way I could find to allow them to swallow their pride, because with Ophelia at least I was very sure that once she was out of her panties and over my knee she'd soon learn to enjoy what she'd taken such pleasure in dishing out. Portia was another matter.

They certainly found it amusing to flick at each other's bottoms with their riding crops, a sight that left had me weak at the knees and in desperate need of a few minutes alone with a vibrator from the start. Each time I had fantasised about giving them the hard, bare bottom spankings they both so richly deserved, and about them growing excited by the treatment and ending up on their knees to me. I'd been the one who ended up getting spanked, and on my knees, but I had at least made fantasy a reality, after a fashion, and I was now confident in my ability to get what I wanted.

That was going to take time, but for the moment I really needed to redress the balance. Being a Saturday there was nothing to stop me from doing exactly that, so long as I could find a suitable candidate whose bottom I could use to soothe my bruised ego. Unfortunately Morris Rathwell had manage to corral all my open-minded female friends so effectively that it was hard to arrange anything without him finding out, and if he did it was sure to lead to trouble. That left a handful of hardcore lesbians, but they tended to be in monogamous couples and the sort of submissive girlies I liked were always in short supply. Yet at the very least they respected me as a fellow domina, so I decided that a trip to the lesbian bar, Whispers, would be my best choice, and there was always a chance that I'd get lucky.

That also gave me an opportunity to dress up, something I hadn't done in a while. It was pointless to try and outdo the butch dykes, with their tattoos and piercings or carefully cultivated masculine style, so I chose a black leather dress that I hoped would give me the strong, matronly look many of the girls appreciated. The cut showed my breasts and hips well, while a pair of black heels lifted me to six foot tall, completing the strong, dominant image I wanted.

Just being dressed like that did wonders for my confidence, and as I adjusted my make-up and checked that I had everything I needed in my bag I was imagining how the day might turn out. I knew several of the regulars at Whispers, mostly hard cases like "AJ" Croft, but a few who were far more my style, while there was always a chance of somebody new. One thing was certain, she would have to enjoy being spanked, because that was what she was going to get. The spanking from Hannah had been just the right dose for me, but since then I'd been punished and humiliated by both James and the girls, quite aside from being driven to distraction by the sight of them in their skin-tight jodhpurs or skinny jeans. Just thinking about it made my fingers twitch, and by the time I was ready to leave the house my need had become a physical ache.

I threw a long coat on over my dress before going to check that everything was locked up properly, but as I was setting the alarm in the shop the doorbell went. Marjory was still around somewhere and I was hoping she hadn't decided to drop in for a cup of tea, but was surprised to find Hannah Riley standing outside.

'Hello, Hannah,' I managed. 'I was just going out.'

'You've time to talk to me,' she said, pushing in.

'A few minutes, I suppose,' I admitted, closing the door again. 'What's the matter?'

'Put the kettle on and I'll tell you,' she replied, settling herself onto a chair.

I stifled a sigh but did as I was told, knowing I'd left plenty of time and genuinely curious about why she was there. Normally I went to her, for a variety of reasons but mainly because I didn't want to start any unnecessary gossip in the village. Just living with Kay was bad enough, although most people were understanding, but it was bad enough Portia and Ophelia knowing that I liked to be spanked by travellers without the rest of the locals discovering.

'Very nice,' she remarked as she looked around my kitchen.

'Thank you. Here's your tea.'

'Ta, love. Down to business. We're being moved on and we need to find a new site.'

I nearly dropped the tea in horror. She didn't need to say anything more, because it was obvious what she was implying, that she wanted to put her caravan on my land, no doubt along with several others. I began to stammer a reply, but she'd already seen the expression on my face.

'Just temporary,' she assured me, 'until the council get us sorted out.'

'Um … it's not really possible, I'm afraid,' I managed. 'I'm already renting the land out, you see, all of it.'

'There's plenty of room,' she said, and now there was a hard edge to her voice, 'and just think, you'd be able to get your little bottom smacked, regular.'

I began to blush, aware of the threat in her words and excited despite myself, but whatever happened I couldn't possibly back down.

'I'd love to let you stay, I really would,' I lied, 'but it's just not possible. I've just signed an agreement for exclusive use of the whole area, for riding practice.'

'What, and you think giving some posh sods a place to ride is more important than helping an old friend out with somewhere to live?'

'No, it's not that, but …'

'All right then, how about you leave the gate unlocked and we just slip in one night. That way we get our site and you get to keep your reputation with your precious neighbours?'

'Look, really, Hannah, I'd love to help, but …'

She raised a hand, cutting me off.

'All right, love, I know when I'm not wanted. We'll just have to find somewhere else, but this one you've got coming to you.'

She was going to spank me, but my bubble of dominance had already burst and I knew I had it coming, except that if Marjorie came into the yard to wash down she could hardly fail to hear the slaps of Hannah's palm on my flesh, to say nothing of my squeals, and all she'd have to do was peer in at the kitchen window to get a prime view to go with the sound effects. I was babbling entreaties immediately.

85

'Not here, Hannah! I'm not sure we're safe. I'm …'

She'd caught me by the wrist, drawing me slowly in with a strength I couldn't resist, and while part of me wanted to give in I knew it was far too risky.

'No, really!' I squealed. 'Hannah, we might get caught! Hannah! Not here! Take me upstairs, if you want to, only in the front bedroom, and …'

'Shut up.'

'Hannah, please! There's a woman riding on my land …'

'I dare say she's seen a brat spanked before now.'

'Hannah! Seriously, I …'

'I'm going to spank you, Amber, and that's that, but don't worry, because I can see the arch and if this woman comes in I'll let you up, maybe. Now shut up!'

I didn't, still protesting pathetically as I was hauled across her knee. Once I was in spanking position I couldn't have stopped her if I'd wanted to. She'd taken a firm grip around my waist, and as it was I felt guilty for refusing her request, while what I was about to get was in a sense a genuine punishment, which is how spanking should be. That didn't stop me from feeling a really bitter sense of humiliation as she lifted one massive leg, adjusting my body so that my bottom was prominent as possible.

'At least be quick!' I begged, and I'd given in to my feelings.

Not that it mattered, because I was going to get it anyway, and in the most humiliating fashion. There I was, dressed up ready to go, looking strong and dominant in the hoping of finding a girl who liked to be punished, and instead I was having my fine black leather dress rolled up my thighs to get me ready for exactly the same treatment I'd been hoping to dish out.

'Let's get you bare then,' she said, 'and then let's get you spanked.'

It was going to be hard, and I was shaking as I was exposed, the dress bunched up around my waist to reveal the

86

lacy back panties I'd put on underneath. I was also praying that Marjorie would stay out of the yard, the more so because Hannah wasn't content to simply have my knickers on show, but had pushed my dress higher still, right up under my armpits to leave my bare breasts hanging fat and heavy beneath my chest.

'And these,' Hannah went on, her massive hand closing on the waistband of my panties.

They came off, without ceremony, tugged all the way down to my ankles, to leave me to all intents and purposes naked, boobs and bum and fanny all on show to Marjorie if she so much as glanced in at the window. Hannah promising to let me up was all very well, but she'd be concentrating on my bottom and might not notice in time, while there was still every chance I'd been seen in the nude.

'There we are, bare as a baby,' Hannah remarked. 'I'm going to enjoy this.'

She set to work on my bottom, a firm, no-nonsense spanking that soon had me wriggling and kicking my feet in my pain. After a while she began to count the slaps, which made it worse for all that I had no idea how many I was going to get. Fifty passed, and a hundred, with my bottom gradually warming, until she'd reached the two hundred, only then pausing to pull my cheeks apart to inspect my bottom hole.

'Hannah, please ...' I began, but shut up, knowing she'd take no notice.

Instead of protesting I contented myself with making sulky faces as she squeezed my spread cheeks to show me off behind. I knew just how I'd look as well, with my bare fanny open and moist between my thighs, my bumhole a wide, rude star, squeezing softly in reaction to the pain of my spanking.

'Another five minutes and you're finished,' Hannah said and she'd let go of my cheeks. 'Can you see the clock on the stove?'

'Yes,' I told her, and she chuckled for the sulky tone in my voice.

Many times she'd spanked me for a set period, making me watch a clock as I was beaten, one of many sadistic little tricks she used to get the best out of me. Another was to carry on the spanking beyond the allotted time, but that didn't stop me twisting my head around to look at the stove. As I did so she tightened her grip. I braced myself, only to realise that she was bending down to rummage in her handbag. I knew what that meant and was once again babbling entreaties.

'No, Hannah, please, not the hairbrush! No, Hannah, that's not fair. I've got a date tomorrow! Hannah!'

I'd begun to wriggle as I pleaded, but there was no escaping her grip and I was left sobbing in frustration and kicking my feet in my panties as she tapped the wicked thing against my cheeks.

'A date, eh?' she chuckled, and she'd begun to stroke my bottom with the bristly side of the hairbrush. 'Some little popsy, is it? You want to spank her and then have her kiss your arse, I suppose, and don't want her to see that you get the same treatment off of old Hannah? Sure you wouldn't rather I came around and dealt with the pair of you?'

I shook my head and was about to start pleading with her again when she suddenly brought the hairbrush down hard across my cheeks. My words broke to a squeal of pain and she laughed, gave me another slap, and a third, to set me gasping and kicking my legs. The hairbrush hurt, and no matter how often I got it I could never get used to it, or save my dignity by staying still as I was beaten with it, which inevitably made her all the more keen to use it on me. This time she stopped after half a dozen hard swats.

'Oh, silly me,' she said. 'I forgot to check the clock. Now let's be fair and wait until the minute changes.'

It was one more torture, making me watch the numbers on the clock display, knowing that the instant the last of them changed her horrible hairbrush would once more be applied to my bare bottom. My wait seemed to last for ever, with me wriggling my bottom ever more urgently and the hairbrush resting across my cheeks, until at last the time came.

The spanking began again, instantly, to a hard, even rhythm delivered full across my cheeks. From the very first smack I was out of control, kicking my feet in my panties and wriggling in her grip, scissoring my legs to show off my bumhole and fanny, my hair flying and my boobs bouncing, a display as ridiculous as it was undignified. As she beat me she laughed to see the state I was in, and the more I writhed the faster she spanked, laying the slaps in with all her force until I must have been cherry-red behind.

I struggled to focus on the clock, hoping she'd be as good as her word and stick to five minutes. It seemed to last for ever, smack after stinging smack, and I'd burst into tears before she was half done, but for all my very real pain and misery there was no denying the reaction of my body. With every smack I was growing more aroused, until when she'd finally finished and slid a finger in up my cunt I was so wet and easy it made her laugh. My bottom was on fire, and while she had stuck to five minutes she'd been applying the hairbrush hard and fast for every one of them, and yet my wet, open hole told its own story.

'There's no dealing with you, is there?' she joked and gave me another hard slap, then began to fiddle with my fanny. 'We'll call that a day then, shall we, seeing as how you need to get yourself off so bad?'

'Upstairs, please,' I managed. 'I beg you, Hannah. A spanking's one thing, but ...'

'Nonsense,' she laughed, 'the way things are nowadays there'd be less remark over you getting a mouthful of cunt than having your backside slapped. All right, if I must.'

She'd begun to get up and I scrambled off her lap as she rose, only to trip over my own panties as I tried to get to my feet, ending up sprawled on the floor in a crawling position.

'Suits you,' she told me, 'stay like that.'

She made for the door and I followed, crawling on my hands and knees with my panties now around one ankle and my bare red bottom flaunted behind me. There was no denying that it felt good, both to be bare and to be spanked as I crawled after the woman who'd punished me. She looked back as she reached the stairs, with a chuckle of amusement and contempt to see the state she'd put me in so easily, but I couldn't even find it in myself to resent her.

Once we were in the bedroom she lost no time, sitting heavily down on the bed and rucking up her dress. I crawled between her knees and buried my face in the warm, musky flesh of her sex as she pulled her knickers aside. She gave a contented sigh as I began to lick and I let myself relax, glad to have escaped being caught during my spanking, while for all my shame she'd got me both horny and submissive. I was fully willing, but she took hold of my hair anyway, pulling my head in to make sure I stayed put and did my job properly. There would be no escape until she'd come, so I puckered up my lips to suck on her over-sized clitoris, making myself comfortable at her feet with my knees well apart and my bottom pushed out.

As I licked and kissed at her sex I reached back to explore my bottom. My flesh was hot from spanking, the skin between my cheeks moist with sweat, my anus sensitive and wet, my cunt ready. I started to masturbate, revelling in my own humiliation as I thought of how I'd been taken in hand so well, brought down from my pose of dominance, my boobs pulled out and my panties taken down, my bare bottom spanked hard.

I'd been in tears, as pathetic as I was ridiculous, stripped of my dignity just as surely as I'd been stripped of my clothes. I'd been made to crawl, along the floor of my own house, near naked with my red bottom cheeks jiggling behind me and my wet cunt on show. I'd been made to kneel

90

on my bedroom floor, grovelling at the feet of the woman who'd spanked me so well as I said thank you the best way I knew, by licking her to ecstasy as I rubbed my own greedy cunt to orgasm.

My body went tight as I came, shudder after shudder of ecstasy running through me, but I never once stopped licking and Hannah held her grip tight in my hair even when I'd finished. I could barely breathe, but I did my best, using my lips and tongue on her big clitoris until at last she gave a long, happy sigh, her fingers twisting hard into my hair and her thighs squeezing around my head as she too came.

As I rocked back on my heels our eyes met and for an instant we shared a grin, both happy in our roles for all that what I'd done was the exact opposite of what I'd been after just a few minutes earlier. I felt better for it though, and was smiling as I went into the bathroom to tidy up. As I began to wash I caught the sound of horse's hooves outside and peered down to see Marjorie Crowthorne-Jones in the yard. She was by the tap, tending to her horse, which meant that had she arrived just a few minutes earlier there was every chance that she'd have witnessed my spanking. The thought of her watching as I lay squalling over Hannah's knee set me cold inside, a feeling worse by far than when I'd actually been getting it and the horror of discovery had been balanced by my arousal.

Yet I'd escaped, for once, but if there had been a fair chance of James not noticing that I'd been punished before, now it was hopeless, as a rueful inspection in the bathroom mirror proved beyond doubt. My bottom was a mess. Both my cheeks were a rich red all over, which would quickly fade, but there were a lot of darker marks as well, where Hannah had caught me particularly hard with the hairbrush. I knew I would be bruised in the morning and that unless I kept my knickers up James would realise that I'd been spanked, and hard. He'd want to know who'd done it, inevitably, which filled me with fresh embarrassment as I

91

returned to the bedroom.

'You've marked me, Hannah,' I told her accusingly. 'I said you would.'

'Worried about your popsy, are you?' she laughed. 'Oh well, if she can't handle getting it from a girl who gets her own, just bring her around and I'll do both of you, like I said.'

I didn't bother to answer, not wanting to tell her about James. Marjorie was still outside, and quite likely to knock at the back door and ask for tea, so I was keen to get rid of Hannah as soon as I could. I'd given up any thought of going to Whispers anyway, and simply threw on a blouse and skirt, with a bra but no panties underneath to spare my bruised flesh. Hannah watched me dress, smiling when she saw that I'd decided to go without knickers but for once keeping her thoughts to herself. When we went downstairs our tea was cold and she demanded more, which I made, all the while with one eye out for Marjorie. Sure enough, the rap on the glass I'd been dreading came, but fortunately she only wanted to ask if I'd like to come over to their house for drinks that lunchtime. I accepted and she went back to grooming her horse, sparing me the embarrassment of having to introduce her to Hannah. My relief was short-lived, as no sooner had I returned to my tea than Hannah once more brought up the subject of brining her caravan onto my land.

'I said it wasn't possible,' I pointed out.

'And I said you could accidentally leave the gate open,' she responded.

'Hannah, please,' I begged, 'you know I can't do that, and besides, you just spanked me!'

'That was for your cheek,' she answered, 'and you'll get it again if I hear any more of it. Now what's it to be?'

'I can't! I'm sorry, but …'

'A great friend you are. Think it over, right? You know where I am.'

She swallowed the last of her tea and hauled herself to her feet. I was feeling guilty as I showed her to the door, but was determined not to give way. She kissed me before she left, which was unusual for her, and treated herself to a last feel of my bottom, which wasn't. I came to the door, glancing down the road in the hope that nobody was about, to find Portia approaching. Hannah read my glance and her mouth curved up into a grin.

'So that's your popsy, is it? Very nice. Good enough to eat, I'd say. Why don't you bring her round sometime?'

'It wouldn't work,' I said earnestly, hustling her towards her car. 'Look, I'll … I'll come round soon, OK?'

'You do that,' she answered, gave another appreciative glance towards Portia and lowered herself into the car.

I'd got rid of her just in time, and she evidently hadn't recognised Portia from their previous encounter, which was just as well. They only had one thing in common, me, and the thought of them discussing my punishments in the street was enough to set me blushing, so that my face was still hot and red as Hannah drove away and Portia came close. Rather than her normal skinny jeans or jodhpurs she was wearing a short, bright red summer dress. She'd also done something to her hair, which made a soft, black cloud around her shoulders, and I couldn't help but agree with Hannah that she looked good. Had it not been for the bossy expression on her face she'd have been the perfect English rose.

'That was the woman from the caravan on Cutler's Lane, wasn't it?' she demanded as she reached me.

'Yes,' I admitted, and as she saw the colour of my face her expression turned to astonishment.

'You've been spanked, haven't you? Don't you ever get enough?'

'It wasn't like that …,' I began, but she wasn't paying attention.

'You're a disgrace! Come on inside, I want to see, and

I've a good mind to give you another dose of the same.'

'We'd better not. I think your mum's still around somewhere.'

'No she's not. I passed her down the road. Did she invite you to drinks?'

'Yes.'

'Well, you're not coming. Right, let's see your bottom. Come on.'

'Portia!'

She taken hold of my ear, in the middle of the street, where anybody might have seen, and all I could do was get inside as quickly as possible and push the door closed behind us. Portia had my skirt up in a moment, laying my bottom bare in the hallway and holding it in place as she inspected me.

'Could you be a bit more discreet?' I asked.

'You certainly caught it!' she said, ignoring my remark. 'And no knickers? Tut, tut. Stick it out a bit.'

I made a face but obeyed, telling myself that I would return every humiliation she inflicted on me ten times over when the time came as I showed off my smacked bottom for her. Her hand settled on my skin, feeling the heat of my flesh and she gave me a couple of gentle pats before tucking my skirt up into its waistband to leave me bare behind as she went into the kitchen. I followed, feeling more than a little sorry for myself.

'We have a test for you,' she said, 'to see how obedient you really are. Do you remember James Sebastian, whom we introduced you to at the Bayden Gymkhana?'

'Yes,' I answered, cautiously.

'You're to arrange a date with him,' she went on, fishing in her bag. 'Here's his number in case you didn't get it at Bayden. Suggest a drink and go in something sexy. He can be relied on to do the rest.'

'And that's the test?' I asked, perplexed and more than a little curious.

'Yes,' she told me, 'and to let him go as far as he likes. We know you prefer girls and don't handle men well, so it will prove your devotion, and when he's humping away on top of you, or making you swallow down his spunk you can think of what a good girl you are. Is that clear?'

I gave an uncertain nod, wondering what she knew, and didn't know, but most of all what was going on behind the scenes.

'You're a slut, Amber,' she said. 'I expected at least some resistance. What are you?'

'A slut,' I told her, and given that I'd already done what she was trying to push me into it was hard to deny that it was true.

'Now for your punishment,' she went on. 'Come upstairs.'

'What punishment?' I asked. 'Portia, I've been spanked really hard, and …'

'I'm not going to spank you.'

'What are you going to do then?'

'You'll see. Come on.'

She left the kitchen and I followed, full of chagrin and acutely aware of my bare bottom, but more puzzled than anything. At the top of the stair she paused, opening one door and then another before going into my bedroom.

'Strip,' she ordered casually as I entered behind her.

I began to undress, wondering what she had in store for me but fairly sure that I would end up on my knees with my head between her thighs, if not with her perfect little bottom in my face, something I could hardly resist whatever the cost. She watched, and when I was nude burrowed into her bag once more, this time to pull out a hank of rope. I realised I was to be put in bondage.

'Get on the bed,' she ordered.

'What position do you want me in?'

'Whatever's most comfortable.'

It wasn't the response I'd been expecting, but I climbed

on to the bed and lay down, half turned, with my wrists behind my back to make it easy for her to tie me up, but my upper body flat so that if she wanted a lick she'd find it easiest to sit on my face. She unwound the hank of rope and put a strand behind my wrists, wrapping it around them to form a cinch and tying it off. I could tell that she knew what she was doing, and closed my eyes as she continued to work, enjoying the sensation of being nude and helpless on my own bed.

She used a second cord to tie my ankles together, slightly to my surprise as I'd expected her to want to turn me fully on my back and make me spread my legs. Yet now I was vulnerable from behind, my reddened bottom bare for her attention, and as she drew up my legs it left my fanny and anus showing. I'd begun to shake for what she was doing to me, and she wasn't finished. Another cord tied off on the cinch around my ankles and passed under the bed left me more helpless still, not only unable to protect myself but fastened securely in place. She even tied the cord off under the bed, so that getting free would be almost impossible, and with that she stood up, to look down on me with a satisfied smile.

'That should keep you out of mischief for a while, although I dare say a clever girl like you can escape eventually. I'll come back anyway, just in case, at around dinner time. Bye.'

She gave me a playful slap across my bottom and made for the door.

'Aren't you going to play with me?' I demanded, but as the door closed behind her I realised that she already was.

I knew she'd be downstairs, waiting until I'd worked myself into a state of submissive ecstasy before coming back to deal with me. That way I'd do anything she wanted, and like it, even beg for it, but it wasn't really necessary. I didn't need tricks to make me compliant, just the thought of her beauty, her cruelty, and at the back of my mind the prospect of revenge. It was good though, to be completely at her mercy, in the nude with my hands and feet securely tied, my legs up to leave my fanny and anus vulnerable, to her fingers, to her tongue, to anything she chose to push up me.

The front door slammed and I found myself smiling, knowing full well it was all part of the game to make me think she'd really left and amused by the way she was so earnest about her dominance and yet at the same time so innocent. It was sweet, and sexy too, allowing her to indulge the cruel tricks she'd learnt with me before the time came to turn the tables, when I'd be able to show her just how cunningly sadistic one woman can be with another.

After a while I allowed myself the luxury of a little squirm, just to check that my bonds really were secure and to enjoy a delicious moment of panic, mild but still real, as I discovered that I was well and truly tied up. She'd done the cinches perfectly, secure without being too tight, while rope under the bed not only fixed me to it but prevented me from getting my feet up between my arms and so bringing the knot that secured my wrists to my teeth.

She was taking her time, and I began to think of making a serious attempt at escape, not because I wanted to be out of bondage, but to show the little brat she wasn't as clever as she thought she was. Inevitably she'd punish me, but that was just fine. With luck she'd tie me up again and then sit her bottom in my face, with her sweet little cheeks spread and my nose pushed to her anus as I licked her fanny. The thought made me shiver and I began to wriggle in my bonds, sure that with enough patience I could get my wrists free, after which it would be easy.

I was also wishing I'd thought of using the loo before letting her tie me up. All the tea I'd drunk was having its inevitable effect, and the pressure in my bladder was beginning to grow uncomfortable. I moved around, grimacing as my attempts to free my wrists grew more serious. It was possible, it had to be, but she'd used ten or even twelve turns to make the cinch, encasing my wrists in the soft, supple cord, while she'd also done something clever with the knot so that my efforts were making it slowly tighter.

Finally I gave up, frustrated, but also excited at my inability to escape. She knew her stuff, even if it had come from books rather than experience, which probably meant she was waiting until I called out for her. That would reinforce my submissive status, or so she thought, but I'd been playing exactly the same sort of game about the time she'd been in nappies. I was rather wishing I was, in nappies that is, because if I didn't escape soon I was going to wet myself, all over my bed. It was far easier to give in.

'Portia!'

There was no answer, which was exactly what I'd expected.

'Portia, please! I give in.'

Still no answer.

'Please, Portia! OK, Mistress Portia ... Lady Portia, anything you like. I submit. I did say I'd be your pet. Come on, Portia, please!'

Silence. I knew she was teasing me. She had to be, but a nasty suspicion was beginning to grow on me. Maybe she wasn't the carefully self-taught and thoroughly modern domina I imagined? Maybe she was just a vicious little bitch who got off on other people's pain and humiliation, and old-fashioned bullying, a vindictive brat like some of the girls I'd know at school.

'Portia! Please! OK, red, or whatever safe word you use. Red! Come on Portia!'

I began to struggle, for real now, the frustration welling up in my head with the rising pressure in my bladder. She had to be downstairs, but my pleas had met with utter silence. I bit my lip as I forced myself to concentrate on the ties, but the pain in my bladder was so strong it was almost impossible to think of anything else. If she didn't come quickly it was going to be too late, and even if she did I wasn't sure I could hold it while she untied me. I began to wriggle my toes, bringing back memories of standing in church in much the same condition, desperate to pee but not daring to leave. Yet I'd always held it, never once ended up standing in an embarrassing little puddle with my Sunday shoes full of piddle.

'Bitch!' I hissed, and I'd finally got the first loop of my wrist cinch over my thumb, only to pull the knot tighter still. 'Portia! Please, Mistress Portia, untie me! I'm begging you, please! Come on, Portia, or I'm going to wet myself!'

I screamed out the last words, now writhing on the bed, genuinely panic-stricken, with the first tears squeezing from my eyes as I tried to decide whether I should wet my bed or stick my bottom over the side and do it on the carpet. Then it was too late, the pain rising once more, too strong to resist and a little squirt of pee had escaped my hole, to trickle down my thigh and onto the coverlet. I cried out, still fighting it, but only for a moment more before I gave in. Sobbing bitterly and with tears of frustration coursing down my face I twisted my body around to stop it spraying all over the place and let go.

The piss squirted from my cunt, over the bed and down my thighs and bottom cheeks, soaking my skin and the coverlet. I was still working at my bonds as it came, but in raw, uncoordinated jerks, each of which made a fresh jet of piddle erupt over my bed, until I was squirming my bottom into a soggy mess of soiled bed linen. Still the pee came, and there was no denying the relief of emptying my bladder, even though it meant wetting myself and my bed. There was no point in holding back anyway, so at last I let myself go limp, to lie sobbing in utter defeat as the rest of my piddle bubbled out from my fanny to add to the mess.

I'd pulled my wrists up into the small of my back when the first spray of piddle came, knowing that if the cord got wet my chances of escape would be that much worse. The movement had changed the tension of my cinch and I realised that if I pushed up and down, each time using my thumb to drag a loop of cord a little further I could eventually escape. I set to work even as the last trickle of pee ran down my leg, determined to get free before Portia came back.

It seemed to take for ever, with my bottom squashing in my pee soaked bedclothes as I wriggled and squirmed, tugged and jerked. I was soon sweating and gasping for air, but the cords were coming down, one by one, worked slowly onto my hands and finally off. With the first three loops of cords off the tension suddenly went and it quickly got easier, so that I was soon lying back and shaking my sore wrists, still with my feet bound but triumphant.

There was still no sign of Portia, and it would have taken just moments to unfasten the cinch binding my ankles and release myself from the cord fixing me to the bed. I wasn't going to do it though, not yet. The evil little bitch really had gone, of that I was sure, because if she was downstairs she'd have known I'd wet myself and I couldn't see her resisting the opportunity to come up and gloat, or maybe even do what her sister had threatened to and piss on me in turn. Not that it made any difference if she caught me or not. I'd wet my bed, while tied helpless, an experience too strong to resist. I had to come.

My thighs came open, as wide as they'd go, spreading my pee-soaked fanny and increasing the tension on the cords binding my ankles to keep me firmly in mind of the situation I was in as I set to work. I closed my eyes, masturbating freely, one hand on my wet fanny the other stroking and squeezing at my boobs. My bottom was in a puddle, my own puddle where I'd wet my bed, the sodden coverlet clinging to my skin as I wriggled myself into the warm, sticky mess. In just seconds I'd started to come, thinking first of how Portia and tied me up and abandoned me to my fate, then how it had felt to be tied and helpless as the pain in my

100

bladder grew and the awful frustration of knowing I was going to wet myself rose to the point where I'd burst into tears even as I let go.

With that thought I did exactly that, fresh pee squirting from my open cunt even as my muscles locked in orgasm, jet after jet of hot urine erupting to splash against my clutching fingers and wet my thighs once more, to soil yet more of the bed and spatter down on the floor beyond. Some even went on my dresser, but I no longer cared, gasping out my ecstasy as I deliberately wet myself and only when my climax had run its course and I'd slumped back down into my pee puddle did I find it in myself to curse Portia Crowthorne-Jones for a vicious, spiteful little hell-cat who needed her bottom pulled out of her panties and smacked for her, hard, often, and preferably in public.

Chapter Seven

Portia was not in my house. Nor was she anywhere nearby. She really had deserted me, which left me both astonished and outraged. Worse still, it was hours before she came back, by which time I'd washed my bedclothes and had just finished hanging the blankets out over the jumps to let them dry in the sun. Even then she didn't bother to apologise, but she couldn't have known I was going to wet myself, so I didn't tell her, let alone give her the bare bottom spanking she so richly deserved. Instead I postponed my revenge and meekly went down on my knees to lick her fanny as she sat sprawled in an armchair in my living room. She was more than a little drunk, and also on edge, repeatedly reminding me that I'd promised to prove myself to her by letting James Sebastian have his wicked way.

Once I'd brought her to orgasm she demanded a cup of tea, but by the time I brought it back she was sound asleep, still with her dress up and her knickers around her knees. The temptation to strip her, tie her up and whip her bottom for her was almost overwhelming, but I once more allowed my morals to get the better of me. After adjusting her panties and taking off her dress to put in the wash I carried her upstairs and put her to bed in the spare room, where she curled up and stuck her thumb in her mouth, fast asleep.

She did look sweet, sucking her thumb with her legs tucked up in the same position she'd tied me, with her little white panties taut over her lovely bottom. I badly wanted to pull them down, and after a moment of wrestling with my conscience I told myself that as a few minutes before she'd ordered me to do exactly that it was OK. That didn't stop me from feeling a flush of guilt as I took hold of the waistband and eased them down her legs to get her bare, so that her fanny lips were peeping out from between her thighs and her bottom hole showed between her perfect little cheeks.

I could have spanked her, so easily, but it wouldn't have been right and it wouldn't have been the same. When the time came she would offer me her bottom, perhaps reluctantly, hopefully with a great deal of embarrassment, but willingly. So I contented myself with planting a gentle kiss on the crest of each beautiful little cheek and one between for good measure, then pulled her panties back up and tucked her in, secure in the knowledge that I was being suitably servile, even when it came to kissing her anus.

She'd stayed away until the end of her mother's garden party, a piece of breathtaking arrogance when she had me tied naked on my bed, so I knew that it was too late to take up Marjorie's invitation and go over. It was tempting anyway, just for the pleasure of telling her that Portia was drunk and asleep in my spare room, and for Portia's undoubtedly cruel and inventive revenge, but I decided it wouldn't be sensible. Besides, Portia had made it very clear that she didn't want me to go, although I wasn't at all sure why. It couldn't be pure snobbery, even from her, and it seemed over subtle for an act of cruelty or a punishment, not to mention having no discernable erotic implications.

It was a minor mystery and I put it to one side, spending the rest of the afternoon doing housework until Portia finally woke up, once more demanding tea, and then orange juice. I provided both, and would have been happy to play, but she was so much the worse for wear after over indulging herself that she only wanted to get home. She even thanked me for looking after her, so she must have felt really ill, and once she'd gone I was left to my own devices. It had been a long day, what with one thing and another, so I made myself some supper, watched TV for a while and went upstairs early, first to cream my still smarting bottom, then to masturbate myself to sleep with a hundred and one dirty thoughts running through my head.

My first thought on waking up was that I was due to meet James for lunch, immediately followed by wondering how I was going to explain the state of my bottom. The obvious answer was to keep my knickers up, but that was no fun at all. Pretending I'd suffered some form of bizarre and highly improbable accident was quite simply impractical, as an inspection of my cheeks would show to anybody, let alone a man of his experience, was sure to realise the truth, that I'd been spanked. I could always pretend I'd done it myself, which would be embarrassing, but quite exciting too, or I could tell the truth. At least, I could tell an approximation of the truth, and as I washed and put on a light summer dress over loose white panties I was sorting out my story.

It had to be something that would turn him on, but which wouldn't make the already complicated situation I'd got myself into any worse, or risk me getting caught out in a lie. I didn't see why I couldn't admit to taking regular spankings from another woman, because while he was sure to like the idea of watching I could explain that she wouldn't allow it, perhaps that she was a hardcore lesbian. In that case I could even admit it was Hannah, because I was sure he would appreciate how humiliating and therefore exciting the situation was for me, but there were other options, which I pondered during the course of the morning.

I set off for the Golden Lion with only a few minutes to spare, not wanting to seem too eager. James was already there, seated on the terrace with a drink in his hand, and even if he noticed that I was a few minutes late he didn't comment. I was feeling nervous and was ready to be taken in hand from the start, but he was as cool as before, ordering drinks and browsing the menu at leisure before ordering

104

lemon sole with an extra pat of butter to the side. The butter came in a small dish of glazed brown china, quite a generous portion, but he didn't touch it at all, leading me to comment when he had finally pushed his knife and fork together and dabbed his lips with a serviette.

'That was wasteful.'

'The butter? Not at all.'

'But you haven't used any.'

'Oh but I shall. It's for your buggering.'

'My …'

I didn't manage to get the word out, the blushes rising hot to my face as I instantly thought of his engorged cock being pushed in up my bottom hole. He carried on, his voice as calm and level as if we'd been discussing the weather.

'Yes. Finish your drink in your own time, then pop into the ladies with the butter and lubricate yourself. Check that you're clean inside too.'

I could only stare at him, my mouth wide open in astonishment and resentment for his outrageous demand. Perhaps I had let him beat me, and held my pose for him to masturbate over my whipped bottom, and I was ready for more, but to calmly announce that he intended to sodomise me took things to a whole new level, to say nothing of telling me to go into the loo to lubricate my bottom, or the final, hideously embarrassing detail he'd added at the end. Yet he knew his woman. Even as a dozen stinging retorts crowded my head I knew that I wanted to do it, exactly as he ordered.

'You are a bastard, you do know that?' was the best I could manage, a feeble sally in return to his suggestion.

He merely smiled and pushed the butter towards me across the table. I sat back, red-faced and sulky, unable even to look him in the eye. As I sipped my drink as I tried to tell myself that I wasn't going to do it, when I knew perfectly well that I couldn't resist. The idea meshed in too well with my love of erotic humiliation, and my need to think of men

105

as dirty, lecherous bastards. He was going to get his way.

I drained the last of my drink, stood up and gave him a look of withering contempt, as if I was about to walk away, but that was all, my single, pathetic attempt at showing him the scorn I should have felt for his disgusting suggestion. Then I picked up my bag and the butter dish to make for the loos with a last toss of my hair, intended to show that I still had some pride but probably seeming merely petulant.

Only in the loos did I give way to the burning feelings of humiliation and arousal he'd provoked in me. The pub was crowded and I had to wait for a cubicle, while desperately trying to hide the fact that I was carrying a dish of butter. Even inside the cubicle I felt horribly vulnerable, sure that those outside would somehow realise exactly what I was doing and imagining their self-righteous disgust at the idea of me preparing myself to take a man's penis in my bottom hole.

I was shaking badly as I put the dish down on the cistern and turned up my dress, tucking it high to ensure it didn't fall back at an awkward moment. Lifting the lid, I pushed down my panties and seated myself, to slip a hand beneath my body. I couldn't resist touching my fanny, just to check that I really was as wet as I felt and to briefly tease my clit. That made it easier, my head now full of dirty thoughts as I moved my hand further back, to touch the tight, puckered knot of my anus.

Already I could imagine the tiny hole stretched open on James's cock shaft, and as I reached for the butter I was tickling my ring and trying to remember the last time I'd been buggered. It had been Morris himself, easing his skinny little prick in and out of my anus as I rode him and his wife spanked me from behind. The memory made me shiver and also made my bumhole contract sharply on the finger I'd now pushed a little way into my ring. James was a lot bigger than Morris and would really stretch my hole, so I needed to be sure I could take him.

106

With my thighs spread as wide as they would go and the dish held under my bottom I scooped up as much butter as I could. The day was warm and it was very soft, really rather too soft, so I had to smear it on my anus and open myself up very gradually rather than push some up and let it melt inside. It was effective though, and I soon had my finger inside the warm, moist cavity of my rectum. My eyes were lightly closed and I couldn't help but enjoy the sensation of having my finger in my bottom hole, because it felt nice but more importantly because it was such a rude thing to do. Yet there was real shame in the sob that escaped my lips as I pushed my finger deep up to check that I was empty, as James had ordered. It was such a crude thing to do, checking that my rectum wasn't full in order to make sure there was room for my lover's cock, utterly filthy and utterly humiliating.

I was empty, which was a relief, but the discovery brought an immediate twinge of disappointment, which in turn left me feeling more ashamed of myself than ever. That didn't stop me keeping my finger deep up my bottom for a long while, nor pulling it out to scoop up more butter and carry on lubricating myself for James's cock. As I pushed a second finger in past my now sloppy ring I was telling myself it was necessary, because if I didn't get myself as open as possible my buggering was sure to hurt, but it was a lie. I was enjoying playing with my bottom hole for its own sake, and imagining how it would feel once his erection had been substituted for my fingers.

It was only when an impatient cough from outside the cubicle door broke my concentration that I stopped. By then I had three fingers deep up my gaping hole and could quite happily have accommodated any man I'd met. After a hasty clean-up and apologies to the short queue which had built up outside I made my way back to our table. James sat as before, a fresh drink in his hand and a faintly supercilious smile painted on his handsome features. I sat down opposite him, grimacing slightly at the sticky, slippery feeling between my cheeks as I settled my bottom onto the bench. He raised his eyebrows.

'I'm ready,' I told him, and pushed the now empty butter dish towards him.

'Good girl,' he responded, 'but there's no rush. I've bought you another glass of wine.'

I gave my bottom a little wriggle to try and get more comfortable, but stopped, sure that the butter would leak into my panties or even stain my skirt. He seemed to be reading my mind, and it amused him, his smile growing broader before he spoke.

'How does it feel?'

'Disgusting … but quite nice too.'

He chuckled and took another sip of his drink, his ice-blue eyes now sparkling with mischief.

'Where would you like it?' he asked. 'In the woods, back at my flat, in my car maybe?'

I grimaced at a sudden picture of how I'd look bent over the seat of his Morgan as he squeezed himself in up my bottom from behind. We'd be blatantly exposed, so much so that the only question for anybody who saw us would be whether he had his cock up my fanny or my bottom. It was appealing, but far too dangerous.

'I'd like it in your car,' I told him, 'but we can't risk being seen.'

'Perhaps,' he admitted, 'but then again …'

He trailed off, his smile now positively wicked. As if at a sudden impulse he drained his drink and stood up, extending his hand. I swallowed my own wine and accepted his gesture, not even sure if he'd paid as he led me to his car. The butter between my cheeks felt warm and slippery as I walked, keeping me firmly in mind of what was about to be done to me, but for all the prospective thrill of being sodomised over the seat of his car I was determined not to take any risks.

'Maybe your flat?' I suggested as he let the clutch in.

'Hush,' he chided, 'I know just the place.'

'But James …'

'Hush,' he repeated, 'or do I have to smack that delectable bottom of yours before your buggering?'

'I assumed you'd do that anyway,' I admitted, 'but be gentle, because I'm a little sore.'

'Oh, yes?' he queried as we pulled out onto the road. 'Not just from the little whipping I gave you, surely?'

'It wasn't a little whipping, it was quite a hard one, but no. I … I got the hairbrush yesterday.'

'Good heavens, you must have been a bad girl. Who from, and why?'

His voice was full of curiosity and thick with lust, tempting me to embellish the story I'd decided on. I'd have liked to pretend it had been a real punishment, but he wasn't going to believe that. Yet there was one person who it was easy to picture dishing out a bit of discipline to me, somebody he knew but wouldn't expect to admit what she got up to even if he dared to ask, Marjorie.

'Mrs Crowthorne-Jones,' I told him.

'Bloody Hell!'

He'd nearly hit another car as he spoke, and after a moment of shock I found myself laughing.

'You're joking?' he demanded. 'I mean to say, goodness knows I can see her as the type, but …'

'She spanks me,' I told him, relishing every word.

'Tell me about it.'

If he'd sounded excited before, now he was almost drooling. It was nice to have punctured his cool for once, and he even seemed a bit worried, so I took a moment to compose myself and then began.

'She spanks me,' I repeated, just for the pleasure of hearing myself frame the words, 'over her knee, panties down and bare bottom, the way a girl ought to be spanked. I generally get it two or three times a month, sometimes more, when she comes in from riding usually, although sometimes she comes round in the evening to give me what she likes to call tears before bedtime.'

I saw him swallow, and was struggling to keep my tone even and stop myself from smiling as I went on.

'I like it, as you know,' I told him, 'but we try to make it as genuine as possible, so I've given her permission to spank me whenever she feels it's appropriate. Often it's when I use bad language, or when she feels I haven't been very polite. Then it's always the same routine, over her knee to have my bottom laid bare and smacked, just with her hand, but yesterday she thought I was being rude to her …'

'Yesterday?' he interrupted.

'Yes, after she'd been riding. All I did was point out that she hadn't swept up the mud she'd left in the yard, but she told me not to be rude and that I was long overdue a spanking. She took me by my ear and pulled me indoors, up to my bedroom, where she put me over her knee. I was begging her to let me off, because I knew I'd be seeing you, but of course I couldn't tell her that and I don't think she'd have cared anyway.'

'I bet,' he chuckled, 'and to think I was making polite chit chat with her at lunchtime. Why, it must have been less than an hour after she'd spanked you!'

'You were at her garden party?' I asked.

'Yes, but never mind that. Tell me about your spanking.'

'Where was I? Yes, she had me over her knee and wouldn't listen to my protests. She turned up my dress and took down my panties. Then she started to spank me, telling me what a rude girl I was as she smacked my bottom. I got in a fuss, but that didn't seem to be enough for her. My hairbrush was on my bedside table and she picked it up to use on me. It hurt so much!'

I paused as he made a hasty adjustment to his cock, which was now making a substantial bulge beneath his trousers.

'She made me cry,' I told him, 'and when she'd finished she made me do corner time, standing in the corner of my own bedroom with my hands on my head and my red bottom on show. Can you imagine that?'

'Yes. Easily.'

'Sometimes,' I went on, now embellishing the story as much for my own sake as for his, 'she takes my panties right off and stuffs them in my mouth to shut me up if she thinks I'm making too much fuss over my spanking. She's says I'm a cry baby, and I suppose it's true. You made me cry.'

He gave a low groan from somewhere deep in his throat and floored the accelerator as we turned on to a slip road for the A1. We were doing ninety before we'd joined the main carriageways, only for him to be forced to slow by one huge juggernaut which was attempting to overtake two others. He cursed under his breath and I found myself laughing.

'You wait,' he warned me, and once more jammed his foot to the floor as the road cleared.

'Do you like the thought of Mrs Crowthorne-Jones spanking me?' I asked.

He replied with a growl.

'She very good at it,' I told him, 'very strict, and a firm believer in never, ever allowing a girl to keep her panties up.

This time he didn't answer, concentrating on his driving as we moved north through the warm afternoon sunlight. I closed my eyes and stretched, now enjoying the slippery feeling between my bottom cheeks and the faint ache of my bruises. Just knowing that he was going to bugger me was enough to make me want to play with myself then and there, and while I've never found it easy to accept a man, with James it wasn't so hard. Maybe that was because Portia had told me to do it, and she was certainly going to be pleased with me when I told her what we'd done, but that wasn't all of it. He was good at taking charge, giving me the excuse I need to submit because he had a knack of making my fate seem inevitable and no guilt at all, not at all like some men,

111

who can still be mumbling apologies and asking permission even as they pump their cocks in a girl's cunt, mouth or bumhole.

We'd covered maybe ten miles before he turned off, on to a smaller A road and then lanes, leading in among the woods and fields of the Chilterns. I was going to make some comment about walkers, only for him to turn the car on to a track running between magnificent beeches and then a second time, past a notice warning trespassers of dire consequences if they continued. It was old and stained with lichen, while immediately beyond a chain-link gate barred our progress. While it was certainly quiet, anybody who happened to pass along the lane was going to get a prime view.

'Over the seat,' he ordered as the car came to a halt.

'Not here! Somebody will see!'

'I didn't say I was going to do you here. Now get over the seat.'

I hesitated, but he'd got out of the car and was hunting through a bunch of keys he'd drawn from his pocket. Obviously he could get in.

'What is this place?' I asked.

'You'll see,' he told me. 'Now get over the seat, unless you'd like your bottom introduced to my belt.'

'Another time, maybe,' I responded and I'd turned to bend down over the seat in the position he wanted me, with my bottom stuck out, still covered but distinctly rude.

He unlocked the gate and pushed it wide, making the ancient hinges groan, then came back to the car, to haul my dress up before settling himself into his seat.

'Bare, I think,' he said, and my panties had been pulled down, leaving my bottom exposed as we drove through into what seemed to be an abandoned quarry.

With the car well out of sight of the lane he stopped once more and walked back to close the gates, all the while with me holding my undignified pose. The sun was shining directly onto my bottom and I could feel the molten butter dribbling from my anus and trickling down my thighs and into my cunt, a deliciously filthy sensation.

'An old chalk pit,' he explained as he pulled down his zip, 'my firm handled the bankruptcy.'

He'd pulled out his cock, which he immediately fed into my mouth as I bent down to take him in. It felt good to have him in my mouth again, and to know that the meaty penis swelling to the motion of my lips and tongue would shortly be going up my bottom. That's one of the best things about sucking a man who's going to fuck me, knowing that by getting his cock hard I'm sealing my own fate, and better still if he's planning to put it up my bum. Maybe it feels nicer in my fanny, but there's nothing quite so gloriously filthy as a good buggering.

I'd already had him stiff talking about how Marjorie Crowthorne-Jones supposedly spanked me, and he'd still been half hard when he put it in my mouth, so I was soon sucking on a rigid pole. Yet he didn't seem in a hurry, simply caressing my bottom as I enjoyed his cock and pausing only to tug my dress higher still to spill out my breasts. I took hold of his balls, squeezing them gently as he in turn caressed my dangling breasts, only to suddenly break away.

'Enough, or I'll waste it in your mouth,' he gasped. 'Right, spread your cheeks.'

I complied, laying my upper body on the warm, hard metal of the car as I stuck my bottom out and pulled my cheeks apart, adopting what must surely be the rudest pose a woman can hold, on her knees with her buttocks spread in her hands to stretch our both her cunt and anus. James gave a pleased grunt to find me so compliant and so dirty, while I could just picture how I would look to him, my bottom well spread, my fanny leaking juice and my bottom hole sloppy and open, well greased up for his cock.

He got behind me, already pressed tight, with his balls to

my cunt and his erection sticking up between my cheeks. I knelt his knuckles as he took hold of his cock, then the smooth, turgid head as rubbed it in my slit, and lower, his helmet directly against my buttery anus. He pushed and I forced myself to relax, but I was still gasping as I felt my ring spread to the pressure, opening only reluctantly to accept him, but opening, first to take the meaty, bulbous head and then his shaft, jammed inch by inch up through my straining anus and into the cavity beyond.

I was panting with reaction by the time he'd got it all in, and in ecstasy, not only for the feeling of him inside me but for the knowledge of what I'd let him do to me and the thought of how I'd look with my big, pale bottom spread in the sunlight and my anal ring stretched wide on my lover's erection. He'd threatened to give me a buggering and now he had, his cock so deep up me that his balls were squashed to my empty cunt.

His hands came down under my chest and he'd taken my boobs in hand, squeezing them as he let his weight settle on top of me and began to move his cock in my rectum. My gasps and sobs grew louder, the motion of his cock inside me grew faster and I was lost to everything but the filthy pleasure of being sodomised. I'd forgotten all about the spanking I'd been promised, but he hadn't. Before long he'd knelt up straight once more, his thumbs now holding my cheeks wide so that he could watch his cock easing in and out of my buttery ring, but only for a moment before he'd started to spank them, turn and turn about and still with his erection moving inside me.

That was better still, spanked and buggered at the same time, and I was sobbing with wanton pleasure as he amused himself with my bottom. Already I wanted to come, bringing myself to ecstasy over both the sensation and the humiliation of having his cock in my anus while he spanked me. When my hand went back to find my cunt he made no effort to stop me, and as I began to fiddle with myself he

114

merely chuckled. That was just right, for him to be quietly amused as I knelt there with my dress around my armpits and my panties pulled well down, my boobs swinging to the motion of his cock in my rectum and bottom cheeks bouncing to the smacks as he spanked me, an appallingly undignified situation to be in, but quite unable to hold back from rubbing myself off.

He let me do it, keeping a steady rhythm in my bumhole and spanking me in perfect time to his pushes, so that it was easy to let my pleasure rise, slowly at first, then soaring to a climax that had me screaming so loudly it startled the birds from the trees and also begging for more. I got it, his body coming down on my back once more, his thrusts growing harder and deeper as he took my breasts in his hands, humping my bottom like a dog with his bitch as my screams rang out around the empty chalk pit. Twice more I came before my legs went, and as I felt his cock pull from my bumhole I thought he'd spunked in me, provoking a last, delightful shiver of ecstasy before I slumped over the seat.

Only he wasn't finished. Before I knew what was happening he'd leapt clear of the car and was holding his cock out to my mouth once more, only now fully erect and glistening with butter and my own juices. I couldn't stop myself, my mouth wide as he fed himself in, sucking eagerly to taste my own bottom as my fingers once more began to work in my cunt, and within moments I'd brought myself to one more, final, climax as he filled my mouth with thick, salty spunk. Even then he kept it deep in my mouth, holding my head firmly but gently to force me to swallow and take what he had to give me down into my belly, eating his spunk as I sucked his cock clean in one more gesture of abject submission.

Chapter Eight

I slept with James that night, cuddled into his body after I'd let him take his pleasure in my mouth, very tame behaviour after my open air buggering in the afternoon but somehow more intimate. The date had gone far better than I could possible have expected, or at least, I had given in to my submissive feelings far more completely than I'd intended to. I'd certainly gone far further than Portia would have expected, not that I had any intention of telling her the juicy details. All I intended to give her was the potted version, that he'd taken me out to lunch, made a pass at me, and that I'd let him have his wicked way.

When I awoke it was to the feel of his cock pushing between my bottom cheeks. He was still asleep, but with a growing morning erection which he'd begun to rub in my slit by pure instinct. I burrowed down the bed and took him in my mouth once more, wanting him to wake up to the feel of me sucking his cock, partly for pleasure but also because my car was still outside the Golden Lion, so I needed a lift. Contrary to popular belief, men are at their most pliable and considerate when they've come, not when they want you.

I got rather more than I'd bargained for, rolled over onto my back, entered and fucked. He was really rather sweet about it, rubbing his cock on my open fanny to check that I was wet enough and taking his weight on his elbows as he eased himself in. If it was a long time since I'd had a man at all, it was far longer since I'd been in such a conventional position, laid back on a warm, comfy bed with my thighs spread to accommodate him, but it felt right. He even went down to lick me once he'd spunked up over my belly, at which point things started to get dirty again, as I was rubbing his mess into my boobs while he took me to orgasm.

As I'd anticipated, once we'd finished he couldn't have been more eager to please. He made breakfast, bacon and eggs, then drove me home with plenty of time to spare. I felt it was time he knew a bit more about me, so I let him into my workroom, feeling embarrassed and yet also proud as he admired my canes and tawses, floggers and single tails, also my harness.

'Ingenious,' he remarked, running his fingers over the smooth leather of my saddle.

'You can saddle me up, if you like?' I offered. 'Not now, obviously, but one evening maybe?'

'I would love to,' he answered without hesitation, 'but, if I may ask, who usually gets to ride you?'

'My girlfriend, Kay,' I told him, 'although I usually ride her, and others from time to time.'

'Really? Someday I must meet your friends.'

'Oh come on, James, admit it, you already have, or Morris anyway.'

'Morris?'

'Morris Rathwell.'

He shook his head, still examining my harness.

'Gavin Bulmer, or somebody from Razorback Paintball?' I asked. 'Monty Hartle? Percy Ottershaw?'

'The names mean nothing to me, I assure you. Who are they?'

'Spankers. You must know somebody. Come on, James, we've slept together, surely you can tell me how you knew I like to be spanked?'

'Ah ...,' he began, looking shifty, only to suddenly brighten up. 'Yes, I suppose I can tell you now, although I warn you it may be rather embarrassing, in the circumstances.'

117

'Go on.'

'I happened to overhear a conversation, you see, between Ophelia Crowthorne-Jones and a friend of hers, ginger-haired girl with glasses ...'

'Gemma.'

'That's the one. They were having a bit of giggle together, and to cut a long story short your name was mentioned in connection with spanking.'

He was right, it was embarrassing, but it made sense. In fact, I couldn't see why he'd felt the need to make a secret of it in the first place, save possibly to spare my blushes.

'And so you asked Portia to introduce us?' I queried.

'How could I resist? It's not every day you come across a girl who shares your passion, after all, let alone a girl so very worthy of the attention. Then of course there were the details.'

'Details?'

'Of how you like it, over the knee and panties down, all that, about how you like to be ridden too, which means, I'm very much afraid – and this is the embarrassing bit – that Ophelia at the least must have watched you being spanked by her mother, and rather more. I take it Marjorie rides you occasionally?'

My answer was a single, dumb nod, because it all made perfect sense, except for one crucial thing. I'd never actually been spanked by Marjorie Crowthorne-Jones, let alone ridden, which meant that Maggie had definitely told the girls about my penchant for pony-girl play as well as spanking. That was odd, because Hannah never rode me, and not only because she was far too heavy for my back. It simply wasn't her thing, or Maggie's. Yet the girls knew, so presumably Maggie must have told them.

'There, there,' James said, placing his arm around my shoulder to give me a soothing hug, 'but you did ask.'

Again I merely nodded, but I was more angry than embarrassed, not with him, nor Portia and Ophelia, or even

Gemma, but with Maggie. Something had to be done.

James left just minutes before Marjorie herself arrived for her morning exercise. She wanted tea, and help with one of her horse's hooves, behaving in her usual mannered but bossy style, which inevitably made me think of how I'd fantasised about her spanking me. It was quite fun really, and provided me with a pleasant daydream to pass what began as rather a slow day, with hardly any customers in the shop and only a single phone call, from Mr Antrobus with another photographic booking. He also told me that he was going to send me some copies of the pictures he'd taken by email, which added a considerable dose of apprehension to my already wanton mood.

What with James, and Hannah, and all three of the Crowthorne-Joneses and an added reminder of how I'd posed naked and filthy for Mr Antrobus, it was hard to think about anything but sex. The photos arrived at lunchtime and I hastily clicked them open, to discover that while they showed me nude and shovelling manure he had selected just five and those probably the tamest of all. It took ten minutes of fidgeting before I emailed back to ask him to send some of the more intimate ones. He obliged, and there I was, naked and sweaty, my breasts looking huge as they lolled forward, my bottom a full, pale moon, but I knew what I'd shown him and I needed to see.

Feeling thoroughly ashamed of myself I asked for the naughty one he'd taken for himself. His reply came after an hour, but he'd done as I asked, sending the picture of me with my face and breasts streaked with filth and my bottom thrust out towards the camera, blatantly showing off my fanny and bumhole. I could only stare at the screen, my throat hot and dry, thick with resentment for what he'd made me do, and with self-reproach for giving in, and for accepting money to pose nude.

I tried to calm myself down with a cup of tea, but it

didn't really work. By mid-afternoon I was badly in need, and hoping that Portia and Ophelia would do something really wicked to me when they came to ride. They came, on time, but as luck would have it so did a clutch of customers, including one of the local farmers who took an infuriatingly long time choosing a few pieces of fencing equipment. Just knowing that the girls were on my land was agony, and by closing time I was in such a state that had the farmer demanded a blow job as part of the deal he might well have got it. As it was he merely kept me on an extra ten minutes before I could lock up, after which I immediately went out to the paddock.

They were still jumping, and while Ophelia gave me a friendly wave Portia barely bothered to acknowledge me. I watched for a while, admiring their smart riding gear and the way their bottoms filled out their jodhpurs, with ever dirtier thoughts running through my head. Finally Portia condescended to notice me, slowing as she passed to ask why I wasn't already in harness. Ophelia heard and laughed, leaving me red-faced as I hurried for the workshop, embarrassed not only for the way she was treating me, but because I couldn't stop myself from feeling pathetically grateful for her attention.

I tried to concentrate on the revenge I intended to take on them, but it just felt inappropriate, as if was the height of impudence for me to imagine myself spanking either of them, let alone the exquisite, ladylike Portia. Rationally, I knew I was just on a submissive high, but that did nothing to dampen my raging feelings as I stripped nude and fastened myself into the leather straps of my harness, making myself a beast for their amusement. It seemed an eminently suitable thing for me to do, crawling near naked and in harness, saddled up for their amusement, while the idea of even attempting to dominate them in any way at all felt like an outrage, and something for which I should definitely be punished. I even considered admitting it to Portia and asking to be beaten for my impertinence, but mustered just enough self-respect to decide otherwise.

My feelings grew stronger still as I bent across my workbench to lubricate my bottom hole and push in the plug of my pony-girl tail. I was still a little sore and a little slack from the buggering James had given me, making me extra sensitive to the plug in my rectum and the tickling of the hair against my bruised cheeks. A glance in the mirror showed me as I was, a fully harnessed pony-girl, my tail in up my bottom, my breasts and fanny naked for inspection, a woman to be used for the pleasure of others, which was exactly how I wanted it to be.

I got down on my knees and crawled back to the paddock, even though they couldn't see me, and they weren't even there to watch me arrive, having decided to take a gallop up and down the strip. For maybe five minutes I waited, until at last they came back, to ride up close to me before dismounting, Ophelia taking the horses while Portia strolled over to where I was waiting, her pretty faced twisted into a wicked smirk for the condition I was in.

'Obedience,' she remarked, 'very important for a girl like you, but what about yesterday? Did you let James Sebastian have his wicked way?'

I nodded, keen to avoid the shame of having to admit to my compliance out loud, with the bit in my mouth making it hard to speak clearly in any case.

'Did you suck his cock?' she demanded, relishing every disgusted word.

Again I nodded, and with that admission I began to cry. Portia's smile grew wider and more evil still. For a long moment she said nothing, simply enjoying the sight of my tears rolling down my face to splash on my naked breasts, but at last she moved on to what I had already guessed would be her next question.

'Did you let him fuck you?'

I shook my head.

121

'No? I'm surprised, a slut like you. So he got over excited and came in your mouth?'

She laughed as I nodded in response.

'But you'd have let him fuck you?'

The tears were now streaming freely down my face as I gave another, feeble nod, and hung my head, no longer able to look her in the face. I couldn't handle the contempt in her voice at all, not when she so obviously found what I'd done with James funny and revolting in equal parts. For me it had been an act of pleasure, between equals for all my submission to his desires, but for her it was plainly unthinkable, a filthy, sluttish performance with a dirty old man, done at her command.

'Did you hear that?' she called to Ophelia. 'She'd have let him fuck her, only he got carried away and came in her mouth.'

Ophelia laughed, a sound as sweet and clear as mountain air, drawing her own pure beauty into yet starker contrast with the state I was in. She left the horses to graze and walked over to us, immediately pushing me down to climb on my back and flicking her crop against my bottom. As I began to crawl Portia reached down to take hold of my bridle, leading me across the paddock. They began to talk, taking no more notice of me than had I been a real pony.

'I said it would work,' Portia stated. 'It's all a question of natural authority.'

'It's because she's a slut and he's a dirty old goat,' Ophelia responded.

'That's true,' Portia admitted, 'but it was me who gave her permission to give in to her needs. She is a lesbian, after all.'

'A slut,' Ophelia insisted. 'She'll go with anyone.'

I gave my head a violent shake, unable to let the insult pass. It wasn't true, while for all the theory Portia had so obviously taken in she didn't fully understand, even had I been the pure submissive she thought I was.

'Only if I say so,' Portia insisted, still ignoring me. 'She needs a Mistress, that's what you have to understand. After all, she didn't go with that guy with the camera, did she?'

'No,' Ophelia admitted as I shook my head with even greater urgency, 'probably not anyway, but she showed him everything, and he's really gross. Did you go with him, Amber?'

'No!' I managed, the word muffled by my bit but not my outrage.

James was one thing, older than me but also handsome and charming, but Mr Antrobus was older still, short, balding, overweight and with all the charm of a traffic warden with adenoids. Both girls laughed, still sweet and silvery but also thick with cruelty, and my stomach had begun to churn before Portia spoke the inevitable command.

'When you see him again, you're to suck him off.'

'No, p ... please,' I mumbled, then spat out my bit, desperate to spare myself the ignominy of what she was suggesting. 'That's not fair, Portia! I can't ... ow!'

'You can,' she interrupted as her riding crop smacked down across my unprotected bottom. 'It's easy. You let him take his nudey pictures, then when he's finished you tell him that being naked for him has turned you on and ask if he'd like you to suck his penis. He's not going to turn you down, so out comes his dirty old prick and in your mouth it goes. Suck, suck, suck, splurt, swallow, and you're done, simple.'

'Yes, Miss Portia,' I said, promising myself that I'd tell her what she wanted to know, which would be humiliating enough but nothing compared to actually doing it, but she was no fool.

'And while you're sucking you're to ask him to take pictures,' she went on gleefully, 'good ones, of your face with his erect penis in your mouth, close-up, and with the spunk coming out when he's done it in your mouth. I want to see.'

'No,' Ophelia broke in, giggling with excitement, 'I've

got a better idea. He might make a pass at her, or he might not, so say that if he does she has to do it, whatever he wants.'

'Yes, I like that,' Portia agreed after a moment to consider her sister's filthy suggestion. 'OK, Amber, you have to do whatever he asks. Now come on, you're very slow this evening.'

She gave my bottom another smack with her crop and I struggled to increase my pace, crawling through the grass as she tugged on my bridle and Ophelia urged me on with the heels on her boots. A tug on my reins and I'd been made to turn, towards the gap between the banks and the sidings beyond.

'It's a shame we don't have two of them,' Portia said. 'We could have races.'

'That would be fun,' Ophelia agreed, 'but I want to try bareback anyway. Whoa, Amber.'

She'd pulled me to a halt and climbed off, to squat down beside me and reach under my belly for the buckle of my girth strap. Portia knelt down to help and again they began to chat, discussing the fastenings on my harness, once more as if I couldn't understand for all that I'd designed and made every detail. My saddle was soon off and Ophelia climbed onto my back again, now with the meaty softness of her bottom pressed to my flesh and her fanny hot against my spine through her jodhpurs. As I started to crawl once more she spoke to Portia.

'I'm not sure I believe her about James Sebastian. He's not some teenager, to spunk up the moment he gets his willy in a girl's mouth. Are you sure you didn't let him fuck you, Amber? Tell the truth, or we might have to spank you again, or maybe whip you.'

I pulled my bit from my mouth so that I could speak clearly.

'I promise, Miss Ophelia,' I said, but my voice cracked.

'I think she's lying,' Portia said and stepped close to

124

touch her riding crop against my bottom, the broad leather tip pressing to my flesh. 'Did James Sebastian fuck you?'

'No. Ow!'

She'd flicked the crop against my bottom the instant I spoke, right on one of the bruises Hannah had made with her hairbrush.

'He gave her a good spanking, I can see that,' Ophelia remarked, craning back. 'Her bottom's in a worse state than it was before.'

'It's going to be worse still in a minute,' Portia snapped. 'Tell the truth, Amber!'

Again the crop smacked down on my bottom and again I cried out, fighting to stop myself from revealing the truth but already at the edge of breaking. I'd started to go red, and I felt sure they knew anyway, because they always seemed to know everything.

'Swear his cock only went in your mouth,' Portia demanded.

I hung my head, in tears once more and unable to speak for my shame. Ophelia spoke again.

'What then? Between your titties? Or … oh no, you didn't? Not up your bottom? You did, didn't you? I thought so! You let him stick it up your bottom, didn't you, you dirty little bitch!? You let James Sebastian stick his dirty old cock up your bottom!'

She broke off in a peel of laughter and Portia quickly joined in. I hadn't said anything, but as Portia took me by the hair and pulled my head back the colour of my face gave its own answer. She tightened her grip as I tried to look down, forcing me to meet her gaze as she spoke once more.

'Did you, Amber? Did you let James Sebastian do it in your bottom? Say it.'

'Yes,' I answered, more a sob than a word, blind with tears as I made my awful admission, but she wasn't satisfied.

'Say it! What did he do?'

125

'He … he did it in my bottom,' I answered, my voice barely a whisper.

'Louder!' she demanded, twisting her hand yet harder in my hair.

'He put it up my bottom,' I gasped, choking with tears as I babbled out the truth. 'He buggered me … sodomised me, over the seat of his car. There, now you know!'

'Gross!' Ophelia giggled. 'Oh hang on, she said he spunked in her mouth … oh no, you didn't, did you, Amber? You didn't let him give you arse to mouth, did you?'

Both girls began to laugh, indifferent to my burning tears and heavy sobs until at last Portia spoke again.

'Don't be such a cry baby, Amber. We know what girls like you are like, don't we, Ophelia?'

They obviously did, to have picked up such a disgusting phrase as "arse to mouth" and there was no denying the truth. Portia let go of my hair, looking thoroughly smug as she stood away and plainly delighted by the way I'd degraded myself, as was her sister.

'No wonder you like to wear your plug-in tail,' Ophelia said, reaching back to give it a gentle tug. 'I suppose it keeps your bottom hole nice and easy for the boys? That's so dirty, Portia. She makes me want to come. Giddy up, Amber!'

As I began to crawl forward once more was she deliberately rubbing herself on my back, growing slowly more excited as she rode me, until she'd begun to moan and wriggle her bottom on my spine. I thought she was going to rub herself off on me, only for Portia to demand a go. She was less turned on but seemed to get a bigger kick out of riding me, making me go as fast as I could with plenty of smacks to my bottom with her riding crop. I did my best, crawling as rapidly as I could manage, down between the banks and into the sidings. Ophelia took over again after a while, riding me back to the paddock, then Portia once more, both now thoroughly enjoying the sensation of having their thighs spread across my bare back and their fannies rubbing on my spine, sighing and giggling with pleasure.

They took turns with me for maybe half an hour, and in all that time neither of them addressed me as a human being once, both giving orders but no more. I'd been used for sex before, but never with such absolute indifference for my own feelings, for all that the state of my own fanny betrayed my excitement at my abuse without a word being said. Even the way they'd humiliated me over James became less important as I got deeper into role, but they were getting increasingly aroused, until at last Portia spoke up.

'I have to come, like this. Slow down, Amber.'

She at once began to rub herself on my back, sighing gently. Ophelia watched, one hand down the front of her jodhpurs and the other clutching at one pert breast, shamelessly playing with herself as she enjoyed the sight of her sister using me. I continued to crawl slowly forward to let Portia enjoy the ride, but she tugged hard on the reins, drawing me to a stop. Again she began to rub, bumping her fanny on my spine, harder and faster. I could feel the wet of her excitement where it had soaked through her jodhpurs, and the softness of her bottom and thighs as she rode, bringing herself high and higher still until at last she came with a sob and a little cry of ecstasy, squirming her cunt on my back.

'Good horsey,' she sighed when she had finally stopped. 'Oh bother, look at me, I'm soaking! What's Mum going to say?'

'It just looks like you got a bit sweaty, that's all,' Ophelia pointed out. 'Get off anyway, it's my turn.'

'Hang on, I don't want Amber thinking we're going soft,' Portia replied as she stood up, and with that she brought her riding crop down across my bottom as hard as she could.

I screamed, and again as the second cut lashed down on my already tender flesh. A third and I'd fallen, face down in the grass with my legs kicking and scissoring as she beat me, six hard cuts in all, delivered to the tune of my screams and babbling pleas, which were entirely ignored. By the end I was gasping and shaking, my fingers locked on handfuls of grass and my mouth wide, my face wet with fresh tears, and as they cleared it was to see Portia pushing down her jodhpurs to thrust out her bare bottom at my face.

'Kiss it,' she demanded and I puckered up on the instant, to press my lips to her pouting anus in a long kiss. 'That's a good girl.'

There was laughter in her voice as she spoke, which broke to a pleased sigh as I poked my tongue out to lick at the tight star of her bottom hole. Ophelia said something, a protest that it was her turn, but I was lost to the world, with my face pressed between Portia's perfect little bottom cheeks as I licked at her anus.

'Good girl,' she repeated, then rose, to leave me to haul myself back into a crawling position.

My bottom was smarting badly from the six cuts she'd given me with her crop, but I was eager to please Ophelia and hoping that I would then be allowed to take my own pleasure, masturbating in front of the two girls who'd made me their pet. My hand had gone to my fanny as Ophelia struggled her boots and jodhpurs off, touching myself in anticipation of what I'd do once they were finished. She had no panties on and I realised that she was going to go fully bareback, but she wasn't stopping at that, stripping off her jacket and blouse so that she was stark naked but for little pink socks and her hard hat as she mounted up on my back.

'I'm going to piss on you,' she announced, and she'd done it, hot, wet liquid splashing on my bare skin even as she spoke.

I could only hold my position, on all fours as her piddle ran down my body, to trickle between my open bottom cheeks and drip from my fanny and boobs, soaking me in an instant. As she did it she was wriggling her bottom and cunt on my back to make the piss splash on my skin and spray out to wet her legs and my shoulders, then higher as she rose a little, deliberately pissing on my head to set her sister laughing in delight. I hung my neck down in utter submission, her pee running down the wet tendrils of my hair and soaking my face to drip from my nose and my chin as she emptied her bladder over me.

'That felt nice,' she said cheerfully, 'and now I want to come.'

She settled herself back on my spine, her thighs well spread to get her fanny to the hard bumps of my backbone. As she began to rub Portia had stepped back a little, to lean on one of the jumps as she watched indulgently, enjoying the view of her naked little sister amusing herself with my body. I held still, the piddle still dripping from my hair and the tops of my nipples, allowing her to use me as she pleased for all that I was desperate to get my fingers to my own aching cunt.

It didn't take long at all. Soon she was sighing and moaning with one hand clutching in my wet hair and the other snatching at her tits. As she started to come she was imploring her sister to watch, then to touch, before her words broke to cries of ecstasy as Portia came over. Ophelia was still coming as they cuddled, with their mouths open together in a long, tender kiss as she rode her orgasm in her sister's arms.

They were still kissing as Ophelia finished and stood up from my back, but I was too far gone to care. Slumping down onto the ground, I rolled on my back and spread my thighs, pushing my fingers into the sloppy, gaping hole of my cunt and grabbing at one boob. I began to masturbate, fully aware that I was lying in a puddle of Ophelia's urine but so lost to decency that what she'd done to me was uppermost in my mind as I played with myself.

She'd been so casual, simply climbing on my back and pissing all over me without even bothering to ask if it was OK, even doing it in my hair, while I was sure that the only reason she hadn't done it in my mouth was because I was the wrong way up. I knew I'd have taken it though, and more, swallowing what I could while the rest ran down my face and breasts, enjoying being soiled by her in any way she chose.

My mouth had come open in mute appeal as I pulled my fingers from my sticky hole and began to rub at my clit. The girls were watching me, their arms still around each other, Portia casually stroking Ophelia's bare bottom. I stuck my tongue out, pleading with my eyes for what I needed, desperate not to give in to the final degradation of having to ask to have my mouth pissed in but failing in seconds. My bit was in the way and I snatched it loose, begging Portia with every filthy word I could think of, to get her jodhpurs down and fill my mouth.

She shrugged, amused, indifferent, but happy enough to give me what I needed. Her jodhpurs came down, baring her neat little fanny and her sweetly rounded bottom even as she sank down into a squat directly over my face. I gaped wide, rubbing frantically at my cunt, my eyes locked to her wet, open sex and the pouted star of her anus. Just to see her like that, squatting over my face as if she was on the toilet was too much and my orgasm kicked in, rising to burst in my head at the exact instant she let go, full in my face, to fill my mouth to overflowing in an instant, with her piddle splashing on my breasts as it squirted forward, a jet so strong she wet my belly and cunt, all wonderful but not so wonderful as having her bottom in my face and my mouth loaded high.

Chapter Nine

Playing with the girls had felt so good it left me wondering whether I should bother trying to turn the tables on them. The idea had felt inappropriate at the time, and while that was no longer the case once I'd come down from my submissive high, it did occur to me that I was having a lot of fun and that I might end up ruining it all. I was far more experienced than them, after all, and surely knew myself well enough to enjoy what was on offer without damaging my self-esteem. That way I could give in completely, as I did to Hannah, and indeed James, while once Kay was back I would have all the opportunity I needed to indulge the dominant side of my sexuality.

It was tempting, but there were niggling issues that needed to be resolved before I could surrender completely. The first was Maggie's breach of my trust, although it was hard to think of what I could do that wouldn't simply end up with me getting my bottom smacked. The second was James and why the girls were so determined that I should continue to make myself available to him for sex. It couldn't simply be Portia indulging her sadism, because Mr Antrobus offered far greater possibilities for humiliating me, and after our session together she had not only reminded me of how I was to behave with the photographer but insisted that I arrange another date with James, and that this time I was to let him fuck me.

Mr Antrobus was also an issue, because while I intended to tell Portia that he hadn't made a pass at me and thus escape my fate I couldn't work out how the girls had known I'd posed nude for him in the first place. They'd seen me with him, and given his large and expensive camera it was reasonable for them to assume he was a photographer, but it was a big jump from there to knowing I'd stripped off for him to take pictures. Admittedly they'd still been on my land, but I was fairly sure they hadn't seen me, while they seemed to know an awful lot, including that I had another appointment with him.

It occurred to me that they might already know him and have set the whole thing up, which fitted the facts but made the whole business begin to look like a conspiracy theory, with everybody in on the joke except poor, abused Amber. After all, it was at least theoretically possible that James also knew exactly what was going on, and perhaps with Morris in the background, co-ordinating everything like a spider at the centre of his web, and a highly perverted spider at that.

In the end I made myself a promise, that if Portia's motives proved to be purely sexual and sadistic then I would allow myself to become what she already believed me to be, her devoted, adoring pet, eager to please and subject to her every command. Just thinking about it sent a sharp thrill through me, because for all my misgivings and my increasingly weak resistance it was something that genuinely appealed to me. It would mean doing whatever she wanted, regardless of my own feelings, including giving in to Mr Antrobus, a thought at once revolting and compelling. First I had to be sure.

Setting up another date with James was another matter entirely, something I was more than happy to do, and to tell the girls about afterwards. I'd admitted he'd buggered me, and every time I thought of how they'd dragged it out of me a little shiver passed through my body, like a mini orgasm. It was hard to see how I could do anything worse, but I was eager to try and rang to ask if he'd like to come over for dinner. He was keen, but couldn't make it until the weekend, leaving me feeling more excited than ever and badly frustrated as well.

I tried to take my mind off things by doing a stock check, but I knew full well that the moment lunchtime arrived my skirt would be up and my hands down my knickers in the kitchen, only for Hannah to appear. She seemed in a good mood, her broad, homely face split into a big grin as she walked over to the counter. We kissed before she gave a quick glance to make sure we were alone, then spoke up.

'I was just passing, love, and fancied giving your tail a warming, seeing as how it's lunchtime and you'll be shutting up.'

'OK,' I answered, trying to sound as calm about it as she did despite the sudden rush of blood to my face. 'I'll lock up and you can take me upstairs.'

She gave a complacent nod and turned to look at my display of dressage whips as I hurried to deal with the door. A spanking was exactly what I needed, over the knee and panties down, naturally, but also long and slow with an orgasm to finish.

'I could give you a serious seeing to with one of these,' she remarked, fingering the sting of a twelve-foot show whip made of plaited leather.

'Just by hand, please,' I told her. 'I'm still a bit bruised.'

She nodded and took hold of my hand, leading me out of the back and upstairs to my bedroom. My heart was hammering for all the familiarity of the ritual as she sat herself down on the bed and I draped myself across her knee in the position I'd come to love so well. Her hand immediately settled onto my bottom, stroking my cheeks through my skirt and I closed my eyes in bliss. It felt so good to be back in spanking position, for all that I'd had more attention given to my bottom in the last few days than in the previous few months.

I knew full well that meant I was getting addicted, but I couldn't stop myself and it was too late anyway. She'd started to lift my skirt, showing off the seat of my panties and tucking it high to make sure I was fully exposed. A gentle pat to each cotton covered cheek and her hands had gone to my blouse, reaching around me to tug open the buttons.

'Better have these out, don't you think?' she said.

'Yes, please,' I sighed, and lifted myself a little to let her free my breasts.

With my blouse open and my bra quickly tugged up my position felt better than ever, both humiliating and vulnerable, and I was so eager I'd gone up on my toes to make it easier for her to pull down my panties. Again I shut my eyes as her big, coarse fingers dug into my flesh around the waistband of my knickers, and I was savouring the sensation as they were pulled slowly down, baring my bottom for her attention.

'Knickers down,' she remarked, 'and off, I think.'

I lifted my legs, allowing her to peel my panties down my legs and off, to leave me bare from the waist down to my shoes and with my boobs showing too, a lovely situation to be in. With my knickers off she gave me a gentle pat on the inside of each thigh, making me spread my legs and show off my fanny behind as she spoke once more.

'I'd better gag you, in case you get noisy. Open wide.'

'OK,' I promised, 'but take your time with me, won't you?'

'You can count on that,' she answered, and my discarded knickers were being pushed at my face.

She'd didn't care whether I was noisy or not, and I knew full well it was just an excuse to make me take my knickers in my mouth, but I gaped obediently to let her cram them in, a mouthful of dry cotton that left me unable to close my jaws properly so that a little scrap of panty material was hanging out between my teeth.

'You are a picture,' she remarked, nodding to the big mirror on my wardrobe in which I was reflected.

134

I could see every detail, Hannah seated on my bed, huge and solid, as immobile as a rock, me laid across her lap, my tawny blonde curls a tousled mess, my mouth crammed with the white cotton of my panties, my boobs dangling low from my chest, the full pink cheeks of my bottom lifted for spanking, the very image of a girl about to be punished. Her hand settled on my bottom, pressing to make my flesh wobble, then applying the gentlest of smacks, and again.

My spanking had begun, slow and easy, not a punishment at all, but purely for pleasure. I relaxed, enjoying the humiliation of the position I was in as much as the smacks now growing slowly harder on my bare bottom cheeks. It began to sting and my flesh to grow warm. My hips came up and I'd let my bottom cheeks apart, deliberately showing off my fanny and anus to the woman who was spanking me so well. At that the smacks grew harder still, each one sending ripples through the flesh of my bottom and legs and torso, all plainly visible in the mirror as I watched myself spanked.

Something was going on in the road outside, to my annoyance, but I tried to ignore it and concentrate on the pleasure of being dealt with so skilfully. Hannah took no notice anyway, but put one bulky arm around my waist to hold me more firmly in place as the spanking got harder still. Now it hurt and I'd begun to kick a little and squirm on her lap, which encouraged her all the more. Soon I was wriggling and bucking my hips, my legs kicking and scissoring to spread out my fanny and show off my bumhole, while my bare boobs were slapping against her fat legs with every smack applied to my bottom.

I was hot behind, my fanny wet and eager, all sense of modesty or decency stolen away as I writhed under her blows, now panting through my nose and chewing on my mouthful of panty cotton. All she needed to do was slip a hand between my thighs and rub a little to bring me off, save for whatever idiots were now shouting at each other in the street. Finally I spat out my panties.

135

'Can't a girl even get spanked in peace?' I demanded. 'Let me up will you?'

'Ignore them,' Hannah advised, maintaining her grip on my waist.

'I can't,' I protested as a new voice joined the fray, shrill and commanding, followed by an angry whinny. 'That's Marjorie Crowthorne-Jones, I think. What's going on?'

'Just relax, will you?' Hannah ordered. 'You're supposed to be being spanked.'

'I know, but …'

I broke off as Marjorie's voice sounded again, louder than before. Hannah was still holding me, ignoring my attempts to get off her lap, but for all that I needed my bottom dealt with, something was obviously amiss.

'I have to see what it is!' I protested. 'Let me up!'

'No.'

'Hannah!'

She'd begun to spank me again, so hard that I was writhing and kicking on the instant, but struggling too, determined to get up and find out what was going on, because there was something about her behaviour I didn't like at all. Finally I bit her leg and she let go, tumbling me to the floor to sit down hard on my hot bottom with my legs spread, but only for a moment. She made a grab for me, but I'd already rolled aside and was on my feet an instant later.

'Come back here, you!' she demanded, but I was already tugging my blouse together as I peered past the net curtains of the window that looked out over the road.

I realised what was going on immediately. Two huge caravans were half blocking the road, Hannah's and another, both pulled by big cars, while three other vehicles were visible beyond, including the truck I'd seen Leary and Sean loading. They were both there too, standing near the gate to the sidings, Sean with a pair of huge bolt cutters in his hands. Maggie was with them, her hands on her hips as she bawled invective at Marjorie Crowthorne-Jones, who was on

136

horseback, directly in front of my gate, giving back as good as she got. Portia was also there and also mounted, but inside the gate and talking urgently into her mobile phone.

'You ... you scheming bitch, Hannah!' I swore as I scooped my boobs back into my bra. 'I said you couldn't use my land!'

'And I said we'd discuss it,' she answered calmly as she joined me at the window. 'What, we're not in?'

'No you're not!' I snapped, frantically refastening the buttons of my blouse. 'And you're not going to be either.'

I'd lost my shoes at some point during my spanking, and by the time I'd retrieved them Hannah had already made her way downstairs. Not even bothering to put on any panties, I followed, to find the front door wide open and the argument louder than ever as Hannah and Portia joined in simultaneously. I ran out, frantically waving my arms at Hannah, Marjorie, Maggie, Portia, Leary, Ophelia, Sean and the entire carload of policemen who had just pulled up.

The police tried to work out what was going on and who was responsible for what. After a moment of highly confused conversation they managed to figure out I was the landowner and all eleven of them turned to me. The police sergeant, a huge man with pepper and salt hair, put the crucial question.

'Miss Oakley, did you or did you not give permission for Mrs Riley to move onto your land?'

I looked at Hannah, who gave back a glance that contained a very clear warning, then at Marjorie, who obviously had no doubt whatsoever which side I was on. There was really no choice at all.

'No,' I answered.

It was not a happy decision. To become the woman who'd allowed travellers into the village would have been unthinkable, regardless of my relationship with Hannah, yet I knew she didn't see it that way. She'd also tricked me, taking advantage of my susceptibility to a smacked bottom to get me out of the way while the others moved their vehicles onto my land. Had it not been for Marjorie and the girls they'd have succeeded and there would have been little or nothing I could do about it, but as it was, and with the timely intervention of the police, they failed and had been forced to move on.

While it was all being sorted out I had been terrified that somebody would bring up my habit of visiting Hannah for spankings, but nothing had been said, even by Maggie, for all that she'd bawled me out with a vengeance, repeatedly calling me a stuck up bitch and worse. She hadn't said anything to Portia either, for all that the situation seemed to have presented the perfect opportunity to drop her in it with her mother, which was so surprising I begun to wonder if I'd been wrong about her betraying me after all.

Not that it really mattered any more. Portia knew what she knew, while it didn't seem likely I'd be seeing Maggie again, or Hannah. We'd parted on bad terms, to say the least, but by the following day I'd begun to wonder if she wouldn't just laugh the whole thing off, at least once she'd calmed down and given me the spanking of a lifetime. I knew that I would take it too, because for all her appalling behaviour I had got my way and deep down I didn't want to end our relationship. Nothing happened, that day or the next, and when I finally tried to ring I discovered that my number had been blocked.

On the Thursday I drove over to where their caravans had been, shaking with nerves but determined to resolve the issue. They were gone, leaving the site strewn with rubbish and me standing disconsolately in the middle. It seemed that I'd gone too far, betraying what had been an intimate if peculiar friendship for the sake of my respectable image with my neighbours, such as it was. I felt so rotten that I was close to tears as I drove away, feeling thoroughly sorry for myself and for once not because I was going to get a spanking, but because I wasn't.

I wasn't really in the mood for Mr Antrobus the following day, but I didn't want to seem unprofessional by cancelling his booking. He was presumably bringing a model anyway, or meeting her at my house, which of course put a stop to Portia and Ophelia's wicked scheme. That was just as well, as while they were keener than ever the incident with Hannah and her fellow travellers had served to make Marjorie less formal with me, but probably not enough for her to take a relaxed attitude if she caught me posing nude for a dirty old man, let alone sucking his cock, being ridden around my land or with my tongue up her daughter's bottom. Just the thought of her turning up while he was with his model was bad enough, but when the doorbell went just as I was shutting up shop it wasn't her but Portia and Ophelia.

'Is he here yet?' Portia demanded.

'Who?' I asked, very sure I hadn't given away the details of my appointment with Mr Antrobus.

'Litenshade, or whatever he calls himself,' she went on, using his web name.

'How did you …'

'By keeping an eye on the photography website you use,' she interrupted. 'You have an appointment with him today at six, don't you?'

'Yes,' I admitted, although still sure I hadn't given out the date and time on the forum, 'but …'

'No buts, Amber, unless you want to go straight over your desk for six with my whip?'

'I think she's trying to get out of it,' Ophelia put in. 'Let's teach her a lesson.'

'We're in the shop!' I protested. 'Anyway, we only said I had to give in if he made a pass at me, and I will.'

'We know you will,' Portia went on as I backed away from Ophelia, 'because we'll be watching to make sure you do.'

I squeaked as Ophelia's crop caught me across one thigh, but managed to take shelter behind a mannequin as I desperately tried to get them to see sense.

'Seriously, girls, not in the shop! Somebody might see, especially your mother, who might well come past.'

'She's entertaining,' Portia replied. 'We're quite safe, but yes, I suppose it's a little unfair to whip you in your own shop, especially if we were to take your knickers down. Leave her alone, Ophelia.'

'OK, I admit I've got an appointment with Mr Antrobus, Litenshade, but he's bringing a model, so nothing's going to happen and it wouldn't be fair on her if you two watch would it? Why don't we have a bottle of wine or something, and I'll make some pasta, then maybe later, once they've gone …'

I broke off as the shop bell chimed again, this time to admit Mr Antrobus. He looked perfectly foul with his round red face beaded with sweat and the evening sun reflecting off his shiny bald pate, while despite the heat of the day he was wearing a grubby-looking woolly jumper, along with jeans that seemed to be having difficulty staying up.

'Could you really make me?' I asked Portia quietly.

'Oh yes,' she said, and Ophelia nodded her agreement.

'Ah, fair maidens three,' he said as he came up to dump the equipment he was holding on the counter. 'Isn't it a perfect evening?'

'Yes,' I admitted. 'Is your model with you?'

'Why, certainly she is,' he replied, surprised. 'You are modelling for me.'

'I am?'

'Why, yes, of course,' he said, his voice rising to a whine of irritation.

'She's only joking,' Portia told him. 'It's just her weird sense of humour.'

'Well I wish she wouldn't,' he said. 'You girls never realise how much time and trouble goes into setting up a shoot, not to mention the expense.'

'But …,' I began, completely nonplussed, only to catch a look and a meaningful twitch of her whip from Portia.

I'd rather have had her thrash me senseless than given in to sex with Mr Antrobus, but just because I was the model didn't mean he was going to make a pass at me. He hadn't done the time before, after all, despite having me naked and alone in my yard.

'She's definitely trying to wriggle out of it,' Ophelia remarked.

'I beg your pardon, my dear?' he said

'Nothing,' she replied, 'nothing at all. We'd better leave them to it, Portia.'

'Yes,' Portia agreed. 'We'll see you later, Amber.'

They made for the door, abandoning me to my fate, or so they thought. I hesitated, wondering if I should tell Mr Antrobus that it was all a mistake, but he had evidently acted in good faith and I didn't want to risk spoiling my reputation. There was also the fact that I had no idea what we were doing, except that it involved a car, which presumably meant cheesy poses draped across the bonnet, hopefully in a bikini or at worst topless.

'…bring the car on to your land,' he was saying and I found myself nodding, my last chance of backing out surrendered.

It was gone half-past, so I busied myself with locking up while he went outside. Given that he wanted me to pose by the car I'd expected something flashy, or at least distinctive, but the vehicle parked over by the gateway to the sidings was a large and ancient Ford, from the eighties if not the seventies.

'Is that the car?' I asked. 'I thought …'

'It is all a question of achieving the right image,' he said, 'but I shall explain presently, if you could please open the gate?'

I did as he had asked, making very sure it was securely

locked behind me once he'd driven the car through, leaving a cloud of ill-smelling smoke in its wake. By the time I'd come through the buildings he had parked, well out of sight of the road but not out in the open as I'd expected but close up under the trees. I watched as he got out, leaving the door open as he began to set up his equipment. Portia and Ophelia were somewhere, I was sure, either in one of the old buildings or among the bushes, but they had hidden themselves well and were being very quiet.

'Should I get changed?' I asked as I approached Mr Antrobus.

'No, no, you're fine just the way you are,' he assured me, never taking his eyes from the piece of equipment he was fiddling with.

I glanced down at my slightly scruffy jeans and nondescript top, wondering if his indifference meant I was going to end up in the nude after all, only for relief to flood through me as he went on.

'A casual appearance is essential for the composition, which is something I've wanted to do for a long time. The moment I saw this space I knew it was the ideal location, private and yet seemingly public.'

'It looks as if we in the car park for a wood or something, yes,' I admitted, 'but that doesn't seem very ... I don't know, glamorous.'

'Glamour,' he said, 'is for the tyro, the dilettante. I create art.'

'Oh. And what does that involve, today?'

'My aim,' he continued, 'it to recreate a licentious encounter in a public car park, dogging as it's called, this as part of a photographic commentary on morals in the twenty-first century. It will be a coffee table book in the end, a limited edition for the discerning.'

'OK,' I answered with a sigh as I realised that it was going to involve taking my clothes off after all, or at the least rearranging them to show off my boobs and bum, 'but

142

what do you actually need me to do?'

'What I actually need you to do,' he said, 'in so many words, is to suck on my penis.'

'To suck on your penis?' I echoed in horror as my worst fears were confirmed. 'Look, Mr Antrobus, I really don't think …'

I cast a nervous glance towards the bushes where Portia and Ophelia were presumably concealed, then continued in an undertone.

'You didn't say anything about sucking your penis!'

'We agreed bg US mag, didn't we?' he asked.

'I don't even know what that means,' I told him, 'and as I said, I certainly didn't realise I was the model!'

'We have agreed our terms and conditions,' he responded, his voice growing peevish once more.

'Yes but …' I began, once more glancing towards the bushes. 'Could you excuse me a second, I need to pee.'

It was the first excuse that had come into my head and he gave me a funny look as I made for the bushes rather than the house, but continued to fiddle with his equipment. I walked a little way up the strip before Portia appeared with Ophelia close behind her, grinning.

'Did you hear all that?' I demanded in a hoarse whisper. 'He wants me to suck his cock!'

'Do it,' she ordered.

'Yes,' Ophelia agreed, 'suck his dirty old penis. Go on!'

'Please, girls! You can do anything to me, and I do mean anything, but not that!'

'Do it,' Portia repeated. 'Think of it as a test of your loyalty.'

'But Portia …,' I began once more, only to break off as she caught my face in one hand, squeezing my cheeks together. 'Ow!'

'Do it,' she said for a third time.

She looked composed, absolutely serious, but Ophelia was grinning like an imp and had one hand pressed to the

143

mound of her sex. When Portia let go of my face I stood back, mouthing wordlessly as I struggled for something to say that would get me out of my predicament, but with my desire for submission already rising in the face of her implacable cruelty.

'Go on,' she said, 'run along and get sucking.'

'We want to see,' Ophelia insisted, 'and you're to do it properly. Let him spunk in your mouth and swallow it!'

I made a face, still weighing up my options, but it was the sheer lust in Ophelia's eyes that decided me. Once I was done with Mr Antrobus I'd be high on submission, humiliated and disgusted with myself, but high, while she'd be excited, and so would Portia. Maybe they'd do what they'd done the last time they rode me, or worse if that was possible, but first I had to show I was properly obedient.

'I'm sorry, Miss Portia,' I said weakly. 'I'll do it, for you ... and for you, Ophelia.'

'Miss Ophelia,' she corrected me, but there was no dominance in her voice, only raw, dirty lust.

I turned back to the sidings, where Mr Antrobus had finished setting up his equipment and was seated sideways in the front seat of the car, the door wide, his little fat legs braced wide. It occurred to me that there was a problem, although it was hard to imagine it was one he'd overlooked.

'Who's going to take the photographs if I'm ... if I'm sucking your penis?' I asked.

'It's all done by remote control,' he said proudly, holding up a tiny black device. 'While the wires you see running around the back of the car go to my laptop, out of camera on the back seat, thus allowing me to monitor each shot precisely. That way you can concentrate on the job in hand, or rather, in mouth, ha ha!'

'This is just an excuse to get your cock sucked, isn't it?' I sighed as I got down on my knees in front of him.

'Not at all,' he responded, sounding genuinely hurt at my suggestion. 'It is a *bona fide* art project, as you will realise when you see the results. Speaking of which, you're very welcome to copies of today's pictures, if you like?'

I gave a weak nod, knowing full well that once I'd completed my disgusting task I would want to see how I had looked on my knees to him as I sucked on his cock, and that I would come back to the pictures for the occasional private moment when I was in the right mood, just as I did to the other rude pictures I'd collected over the years.

'Yes, like that,' he instructed, 'but try and look a little more eager. Remember, this is an exciting, sexy encounter. You're outdoors, in public, and you're about to take a strange man in your mouth!'

He was certainly enthusiastic enough, for all this artistic pretence, his legs well spread to show off the small bulge in the crotch of his jeans. I forced a smile and the camera flashed, recording me in my humiliating position, quite obviously about to give a dirty old man a blow job, but only the start.

'Now put your hands to my zip,' he instructed.

I did as I was told, imagining the girls trying to suppress their sniggers as I was put through the appalling regime. Again the camera flashed and again he spoke.

'Good. Now squeeze my cock and balls with one hand … your right hand so it shows clearly in the picture, yes, like that, and draw my zip slowly down. No, not like that. You need to hold it between finger and thumb. It is crucial that the viewer can see what you're doing.'

Again I did my best to comply, despite a shiver of revulsion as I touched the squashy mass of his genitals beneath the denim of his jeans. Once more the camera flashed, this time recording me feeling up the dirty old man's cock and balls through his trousers as I unzipped him.

'Good,' he repeated, after a glance at his laptop, 'you're learning. Now, pull out my cock and balls. Make sure they're showing properly, of course, and you may need to do it a few times before we get it right.'

I swallowed, trying to fight down my disgust and keep the eager smile on my face as I reached out for his fly. He was looking down at me, and if the pleasure on his face was posed he was a very good actor. As I glanced up the camera had flashed again, again as I drew down his zip, and again as I burrowed my hand in to the big, greyish Y-fronts beneath to scoop out his genitals.

He was small, and wrinkly, and brown all over save for where the tip of his helmet had begun to peep out from his foreskin, bright pink and slightly moist. Men's genitals are hardly the prettiest of sights at the best of times, but his were among the least appealing I'd ever seen. They were still going in my mouth.

'Again,' he said, 'and do try and look cheerful, Amber. From the expression on your face anybody would think you were being forced to do this, and that's not what I want at all. Come, come, you're a woman, with woman's needs, what could be better than a chance to suck on a nice big cock?'

I gave him a brief look of astonishment, wondering if he could really be that self-deluded, but said nothing. He had put his cock and balls back and zipped up, readying himself for exposure once more. I drew in my breath and got on with it, pulling down his zip and extracting his little brown balls and tiny cock from the recesses of his underpants as he took photographs.

'Better,' he announced as I looked up once more, 'but let's try it again.'

Five more times I was obliged to run through the same dirty procedure before he was satisfied. By then his cock had begun to swell, with the fat little helmet poking out from his foreskin, red and wet. The thought of putting it in my mouth made me retch, but I was too deep in to stop, the very humiliation of the situation I was in now bringing up my arousal.

'I think it would be good if you were to show a little

modesty at this point,' he was saying, 'reluctance even, to show that you need to conquer your social conditioning before you can give in to your true, feminine needs. Stroke my balls and make a ring of your forefinger and thumb to wank my cock.'

I gave a dumb nod and set to work, tickling and teasing his balls as I tossed his cock in the ring of my fingers. He didn't seem very sensitive, growing only slowly to my touch, but then he seemed to be paying as much attention to his equipment as to me. I gave his balls a squeeze and began to tug harder, determined to get him off as quickly as possible. My efforts were rewarded with a low moan and several flashes of the camera, only for him to suddenly curse.

'Damn! What a fool you are, Paul Antrobus! I completely forgot to tell you to lift your top. Back to the beginning I'm afraid, my dear.'

'What!? Couldn't I just lift it now?'

'I'm afraid not. The exposure of your breasts is an essential part of the composition, as …'

'OK, fair enough, guys like topless blow jobs, but surely it's feasible that you let me get you a bit excited before you asked me to show you my tits?'

'Hmm, maybe … no, sorry, we'll have to start again. Top up, please.'

We did, repeating the entire procedure, only this time starting with me pulling up my top and bra to show him my boobs before I got to work on his cock. Whatever his artistic pretensions one thing was becoming very plain, that he saw sex purely from a male perspective, with the woman's job solely to use her body to please the man. My own pleasure was presumably supposed to come from making a tart of myself, but the awful thing was that the deep humiliation of doing so, for him, in front of the girls and so slowly, was getting to me badly. I was wet between my legs and my nipples were hard, leading him to compliment me on them when my tits came out, and to grab a quick feel before demanding the addition of one more rude detail to the show, putting his cock between them.

I let him, forcing myself to smile as he rubbed his cock in my cleavage for another six photographs before he was satisfied, which left me sitting back on my haunches, my boobs in my hands, his cock now half-erect, the wrinkly shaft grown taut and silky, the wet red helmet fully out and distended with blood. A glance at my watch showed that we'd been at it for nearly an hour, enough time to suck a dozen men off, normal men, but not Mr Antrobus. He was only half erect, and going down again as he made some fiddly adjustment to his laptop in the back of the car.

'It's going very well, don't you think?' he said as he leant forward once more. 'Now then, we come to the point at which you take me in your mouth and I need to try several different styles. Firstly, a demonstration of admiration, or we might even say worship, in a pagan sense, a woman thanking a man for the joy he can bring. Kiss my knob.'

He had a delightful way of putting things, and I had to hide a grimace before going forward to plant the very gentlest of pecks on the tip of his cock. Inevitably he wasn't satisfied and I was made to do it again, four times.

'Next,' he went on, 'expressions. Try revulsion first, the face of a girl who has been taught that to take a man's penis in her mouth is a degraded act but has been persuaded to do it anyway. Ah, yes, perfect! Who would believe you were acting?'

I wasn't, allowing my face to screw up entirely of its own accord as I opened my mouth to finally take in his cock. He tasted salty, and not altogether clean, so that it took all my will power to hold my pose, now on all fours and leaning forward to suck him as the camera flashed again and again.

'Hmm, don't overdo the look of disgust, Amber, but yes, I think we have a useful shot there. Now, delight, the face of a sex-starved nymphomaniac sucking her first cock in a month! No, you just look mad. Come on, excitement, desire!'

I did my best, trying to let my arousal show through and finally satisfying him by playing with my tits as I gulped him in. This time he didn't stop me, letting me suck as he took picture after picture, with his cock swelling slowly in my mouth, until finally he pushed me back with a heavy sigh.

'That does feel rather nice, doesn't it, but we mustn't give way to pleasure. Focus, Amber! Now then, a more spiritual look, rapture as you lick at the staff of life, mouth wide, tongue well extended! Then you can get sucking.'

He was very nearly erect, and I gave him a few quick tugs while rubbing his knob with my thumb, a sure fire way to get a man hard, before leaning down once more to lick the way he had asked. More pictures were fired off, and still more as I took him in my mouth, now sucking properly on a little, hard erection. I was also playing with my tits, and for all my chagrin and self-disgust starting to enjoy myself. So was he, pushing himself up into my mouth to make me take him deeper and pressing the remote control more or less at random. I wondered if I would simply be given a mouthful of spunk and that would be that, but he proved to be a photographer first and a lecherous old pervert second, pulling me back without coming.

'Nearly there,' he puffed. 'Now, back between those lovely big boobies for a bit, then for the money shot!'

I nodded, now eager, and crawled closer to take his cock between my tits. He began to fuck in my cleavage, his knob bobbing up and down between the fat pink pillows of my breasts, now glossy with my spit and so engorged it had gone purple. Again I thought he was going to spunk, and it would have made a good picture, but again he pushed me back after a few shots, now panting with excitement and exertion as he spoke.

'I can't hold back much longer, so we'd better do the

come shot. We only get one chance, so let's get it right, eh? I think … hang on a moment …'

He broke off to swallow down the drool which had been building up in his mouth, which I could see because some had begun to run down over the edge of his lip. His skin was also wet with sweat and redder than ever, making him look like a little fat devil as he sat there with his legs wide and his erect cock and rounded ball sack protruding from his fly.

'Right,' he said, after a while, 'one chance, so let's make it good. It's all about impact, you see, so I want to capture the moment my ejaculate comes out around your lips, and you will need to show an expression of disgust, thus reinforcing the dichotomy between how women are obliged to behave, as sexual creations of the male ego, and how they actually feel, as autonomous, self-willed beings.'

I could have told him how I felt, confused: ashamed and excited, angry with myself and weak with submissive desire, revolted by what I'd done and what I was about to do, but at the same time pathetically eager to please. Autonomous and self-willed didn't come into it. I was Portia's plaything, and because she wanted it, his as well.

'Now suck me off,' he ordered, and I got down to business.

From the moment I'd taken him back in my mouth he'd begun to push deep, fucking in my throat, while his hand had locked in my hair to keep me in place. I was starting to gag, and wondering how his precious picture would look if I was sick all over his cock. He was certainly taking enough pictures, the flash going again and again until I was half blind as well as choking. Then he came, without the slightest warning, his cock erupting a wad of spunk down my throat, a second, and a third, with his grip tight in my hair and my face held down hard against his balls the bulge of his belly.

I couldn't have held it in if I'd wanted to, much less swallowed it all. Spunk exploded from around my lips, just the way he'd wanted it to, but also from my nose, spattered his jumper and trousers, his balls, and also my face as I fought to pull back. I heard his grunt of ecstasy, my head was jammed back down on his cock, I felt his knob push into my throat once more, feeding me yet more spunk, most of which came out of my nose this time before he finally let go of my hair.

'That was good,' he sighed, 'you sweet little bitch.'

I tried to answer, but only succeeded in producing a wet burp and a great bubble of spunk, which broke and fell to land on my tits with a wet plop. More followed as I began to retch, running wet and slippery down my cleavage and over my belly, mixed with my spittle and the snot from my nose, which was all over my face, while a considerable amount was hanging from my chin in a beard of spunk and mucus. The camera flashed one more time.

'One for the out takes,' he chuckled.

'You bastard,' I managed, but he didn't seem to hear, once again fiddling with his laptop for all that his cock and balls were still hanging from his open fly with his mess and mine dripping down and soaking slowly into his trousers and the ground beneath.

'Excellent!' he declared. 'In fact, a classic, thank you!'

'My pleasure,' I answered, trying to sound sarcastic but not really succeeding. 'Don't you want to clean up? I do.'

'Ah, yes, quite,' he responded. 'You run along. I'll be with you in a minute.'

I went to the tap, to clean my face and chest. My top and bra were only slightly soiled and I decided they could wait, if only because Portia and Ophelia were sure to want to do something truly filthy to me after what they'd seen. I was still tidying myself up when Mr Antrobus appeared, now decent but for the wet patch around his crotch and holding his camera.

'I'll download the pictures onto your computer if I may?' he asked. 'That way you will have copies, while it's always useful to make a back-up as soon as possible in case anything goes wrong.

'That's fine,' I told him. 'It's on, so just put them on the general account.'

He nodded and started for the house, muttering to himself as he went, apparently oblivious to my feelings for what I'd just done. I wasn't, anything but, and I urgently needed to justify myself by knowing that Portia and Ophelia had been watching, so the moment he was out of sight I made for the sidings once more.

'Portia?' I called softly. 'Ophelia?'

There was no response and I moved further down the strip, wondering what had become of them, only to find out as I rounded one of the big oaks. They were a few yards away, in among the trees. Portia was holding onto the trunk of a young beech, her eyes closed in ecstasy, her jodhpurs down at the back, her bottom, pert and round and thrust out full into her sister's face, while it was quite obvious where the kneeling Ophelia had her tongue, deep in up the same tight little anus I loved to kiss and lick.

They hadn't seen me, and I watched in astonishment and ever mounting arousal as Ophelia licked at her sister's bottom, the full details of what was going on slowly sinking in. Portia was masturbating, her one hand down between her thighs to play with herself as she was licked between her cheeks, while her blouse was undone to leave her tiny breasts naked to the air. Ophelia also had her top open and her jodhpurs down, exposing the trim curves of her own bottom with her cheeks spread to show off the tight dimple of her anus and her pouted cunt, with her fingers busy between her sex lips. I had to lick her.

I got down, meaning to wriggle in under Ophelia's bottom so she could sit on my face to have her cunt and anus licked while she in turn licked out her sister. It would have been bliss, not just to have her sweet little bottom in my face one more time but to confirm my position at the bottom of the pile, literally, with my tongue in one girl's anus while

152

she had hers in another's. Unfortunately they saw me and immediately pulled apart, both blushing hot on the instant.

'You didn't see that,' Portia said, trying to sound stern.

'We ... we got a bit carried away,' Ophelia explained, 'watching you.'

'I don't mind,' I told them. 'I was going to join in.'

Portia glanced at Ophelia, then at her watch.

'Um ... later, maybe. We really ought to get back.'

'You took so long!' Ophelia added.

'I know,' I agreed. 'He took for ever, but don't you want to play? He's indoors, putting the pictures on my computer, so we're quite safe, at least if we're quick. I want to make you come, and I need it too, after that!'

'I bet you do,' Ophelia answered. 'You should have seen yourself, with his spunk all over your face! OK, bums and pussies, but be quick, we're late already.'

Portia nodded and took hold of the tree once more, her bottom thrust out, but instead of going down to lick her sister's anus, Ophelia got into the same position and it was me who was left to kneel in the dirt. I didn't hesitate, on my knees in an instant, first to kiss Portia's bottom and then to bury my face between her cheeks, first licking at her cunt and then higher. She'd already begun to masturbate again as my tongue went in up her already sloppy bumhole. I let my hand stray to Ophelia's bottom as I licked Portia's, to tease her anus and sex, concentrating completely on their pleasure.

In no time at all Portia had begun to moan, while she'd cuddled up to her sister once more and her fingers were working fast in her cunt. She came, her cheeks contracting hard in my face and her anus tight on my intruding tongue, where I kept it until she was done. Ophelia immediately grabbed me by the hair, pulling me between her own bare bottom cheeks for the same treatment. My tongue went up her hole and I was licking, already in ecstasy for being made to give them analingus for all that I hadn't so much as

153

touched my own sex. She too came, crying out and grinding her bottom into my face as she clung tight to both Portia and the tree, then relaxing with a long sigh. I pulled back, eager for my own pleasure, my hands going straight to the button of my jeans.

'I'll kneel. You can whip me, or ride me,' I offered, 'or both, anything you like. I mean that, anything.'

'Sorry, no time,' Portia answered, struggling her jodhpurs up around her hips, 'but look, you're seeing James Sebastian at the weekend, aren't you?'

'Yes, but Portia, I …'

'Make sure he takes you out to the paddock,' she carried on, interrupting me. 'Let him have a ride or something, but make sure it gets good and dirty. We want to watch.'

'That's fine, of course, but …'

'Just frig yourself off or something,' she snapped. 'We've got to get back.'

'Just a few minutes, please!' I begged

'We can't, sorry,' Ophelia said. 'Get what's-his-name to lick you out if you need it that badly.'

'Ophelia! What's the matter anyway? Surely …'

'It's Mum,' she explained. 'She's got a dinner party on. We have to wait on table and we're already late. We'll …'

'Ophelia!' Portia hissed. 'Shut up!'

With that they were gone, running off to leave me still kneeling in the dirt, my trousers half down, my mouth wide in shock and frustration, left there to masturbate after I'd taken a dirty old man in my mouth for their pleasure, after I'd stuck my tongue up their bumholes, after I'd offered to let them do anything they pleased with me.

'You little bitches,' I mouthed, but my hand was already down my panties.

My cunt was soaking, and the first touch to my clitoris sent a shock through me that made me gasp. One jerk and I'd pulled my boobs out again, the way I'd been for Mr Antrobus while I'd been sucking his cock, a topless slut on a

154

dirty old man's prick, licking and kissing at his ugly little cock and balls, letting him feel my breasts, letting him titty fuck me, letting him spunk up in my mouth. All of it had been for Portia and Ophelia, every tiny, filthy detail, and when I'd finished I'd willingly licked both their bottom holes to help them come, only to be abandoned, kneeling alone in the dirt as I brought myself to a climax so strong I nearly fainted.

Chapter Ten

I did not ask Mr Antrobus to lick me out. Once I'd come he was no more appealing than he had been in the first place, while the memory of sucking him off only made me feel sick. It had been a superb orgasm, and I knew full well that it wouldn't have been nearly as good if it hadn't been for what we'd done together, but without the girls I wouldn't have done it at all. Portia and Ophelia were what mattered, even if they chose to desert me when I needed them most urgently, although for all the ecstasy it had given me while I was masturbating, their callous attitude rankled as I walked back to the house. After all, it would only have taken a few minutes to deal with me, and helping out at their mother's dinner party couldn't be all that important.

When I got indoors Mr Antrobus was still seated at my computer, looking rather as if he'd been stuffed with his face set in a look of acute constipation. He didn't seem to have noticed me and I gave a discreet cough before pulling up a chair beside him. I'd expected him to have one of the pictures up on the screen, no doubt something particularly rude, but he seemed to be running some sort of program and as he saw me he began to shake his head slowly from side to side.

'Is everything all right?' I asked.

'No,' he responded, 'it is not. You've been hacked.'

'Hacked!? How do you mean?'

'Hacked,' he repeated. 'You computer broken into, not physically, you understand, electronically.'

156

'I know what hacked means, but who by? How!?'

'Very easily,' he told me. 'You security system is, and I mean no insult when I say this, feeble.'

'But what's happened? It's been slow, but otherwise fine.'

'It has been slow, my dear, because somebody, the hacker, has been watching your every move, probably recording every stroke you make on the keyboard, quite possible watching every picture or piece of text you bring up on the screen, certainly going through your files.'

'What!?' I demanded, thinking of all the highly compromising pictures I had, of everything from me posing nude to being spanked in a public bar. 'Shit!'

'Do you keep your bank account details on here?' he asked.

'No,' I told him, with some relief, 'just … just pictures and things.'

'That's something,' he said, 'because nine-hundred and ninety-nine times out of a thousand that's what they're after, but in this case there are some unusual features, distinctive even, as if the hacker had some personal interest in you. Note, for example …'

He went on, and as he spoke his voice grew ever higher and more nasal, but I was no longer bothered with his irritating idiosyncrasies. I let him explain, pointing out to me what had been done and even which pictures had been accessed, including some of the very rudest, which left me red-faced but grateful.

'…a remarkable portfolio,' he said when he'd finally finished, 'and I can see why you like to keep them private. Would you like to know who is responsible?'

'Yes, very much so.'

'Well then, I shall do my best, but please appreciate that it is not easy. Indeed, very few people would even know where to start, but with Paul Antrobus on your side …'

His voice trailed off as his fingers began to move on the

keyboard with impressive speed. I watched for a moment, then stood away. Obviously it was going to take a while and there was nothing I could do to help, except perhaps make the coffee. I did so, and when I came back with two steaming mugs in my hands he was already sitting back in the chair, looking thoroughly pleased with himself. On the screen in front of him was a page from one of the social networking sites, showing a pictures of a slim, red-haired girl with big glasses, also a name.

'Your hacker,' Mr Antrobus announced. 'Geekygirl93, otherwise known as Anderson, Gemma.'

'Gemma,' I echoed.

It made sense, perfect, awful sense. If Gemma had hacked into my computer she, and Portia and Ophelia, knew everything about me, or at least everything that could be gleaned from my collection of pictures and my emails, which was plenty. It even explained why they had assumed I was so submissive, because there were far more pictures taken of me having rude things done to me than of me dishing it out. Morris makes a point of sending them to me, and the more humiliating the situation I'm in the more likely he is to send them.

Portia, Ophelia and Gemma hadn't needed to talk to Maggie, or anybody else. Once they'd known that Hannah spanked me and that the treatment turned me on the rest had been easy, as least for Gemma. Looking at her internet presence it was obvious that she was brilliant, and twisted. Even her choice of music suggested a dark mind, while her sense of humour was frankly sick. She also listed her best friend as Portia Crowthorne-Jones and I could see why. They made a fine pair.

They were going to make a fine pair with their noses up against my living room wall and their bare bottoms the colours of over-ripe cherries if I had anything to do with it. The instant I'd learnt the truth my submissive feelings for

158

Portia had dissolved completely, to be replaced by a burning determination to get even. It wasn't just that they'd been so sneaky either. I could have coped with that, if it had been for the sake of making me their plaything, but they hadn't even had the decency to keep things to themselves.

Pictures had been passed around, pictures of me being spanked across Melody Rathwell's knee, pictures of me being ridden in full harness including my tail, even one of my kneeling on the floor of Morris' bathroom, stark naked with my head held down in the toilet bowl and a tube up my bottom as I was given an enema. They'd had it, and any bleating about being purely dominant was going to get short shrift.

Unfortunately I could hardly march in to Marjorie Crowthorne-Jones' dinner party and spank her daughters in front of her and the guests, tempting though it was. I had to get rid of Mr Antrobus too, because although I was genuinely grateful, once he done his stuff he was in the way, chortling over my pictures and trying to explain the technical details of Gemma's attack on my computer at the same time. He also offered to improve my security system and that did seem sensible, so I let him get on with it, brooding over a bottle of wine in the corner while he tapped away at my keyboard.

It was almost midnight before he'd finished and I was on the edge of sleep, too exhausted to take much in as he explained what he'd done. He also left my money for the photoshoot on the mantelpiece as if he were paying a prostitute, a gesture that at any other time would filled me with mixed emotions and probably made me want to come once more, but now barely registered. Once he'd left it was all I could do to undress and flop into bed, and for my whirling, bitter thoughts I was soon asleep.

Waking was not a pleasant experience, with little chunks of memory lining up for my attention, each one helping to rebuild my seething emotions of the day before. By the time

I was washed and dressed I was having trouble keeping my breathing even, and when I heard the whinny of a horse from the paddock I was immediately looking around me for something to take to Portia and Ophelia's bottoms.

It wasn't them at all, but their mother, who came in for a cup of tea when she had finished her ride. As we talked together I considered telling her everything, but only for a moment. However appalling her daughters' behaviour had been, my own involvement was far too embarrassing, while bringing it all out in the open would also have made it next to impossible to give them what they deserved, heavy and intensely sexual punishments, just as they had dished out to me, or worse.

There was no question in my mind that they did deserve it. No other response suited their crime, while there was no denying that despite everything they turned me on as few others ever had, just not in the same way as before. There was Gemma too, who I'd never so much as touched, but I needed to, badly. Ophelia would get it as well, for all her guileless manner, but whatever I did to them it would be mild besides what I dished out to Portia herself.

She was the ringleader, that was abundantly clear, not only because her little sister deferred to her but from the online evidence Mr Antrobus had dredged up for me. Gemma did the technical work, Ophelia provided the raw enthusiasm for all things dirty and cruel, all three added their own imaginative touches, but Portia was the one who made it happen, the driving force behind it all. There was more too, as I read deeper into their network messages, something going on in the background that they specifically did not discuss online, something very private. I couldn't imagine what it was, but it clearly involved me, which I found positively sinister.

Now more determined than ever, I spent most of the morning plotting and stoking my outrage by following the trails they'd left on the net. By lunchtime I'd decided what to do and how to go about it, a scheme that would hopefully allow me to find out everything I wanted to know, give me my first taste of revenge and put me on the road to more. I would find Gemma, not difficult now that I knew so much, and point out to her that if any girl had ever deserved a good spanking it was her.

There was only one drawback. The temptation to put her over my knee by main force was considerable, but that was against my principles, regardless of her own lack of morality, so she had to agree to being punished. Yet even if she refused I would be able to move on to the next stage of my plan. Portia would be furious, and I knew exactly how she would react. She was extremely possessive, not in the sense of trying to keep her intimate friends to herself, but in the way she had to always be in charge. When she found out that I'd tried to make Gemma accept a spanking she would want to punish me, and when she did she was going to learn that, whatever the books might say, dominance is not all in the mind, and spanking a girl who was trying to spank me was not against my principles, not at all.

A little more dabbling on the internet, a quick glance at the phone book, and I had Gemma's address, a detached villa just outside Bayden. Simply driving over, knocking on the door and demanding justice was pointless, as on a Saturday afternoon I was more likely than not to find Mr and Mrs Anderson at home and they were hardly going to allow me to spank their daughter. Yet I needed to do something and quickly decided to have a look at the area. I was also conscious of the possibility of being recognised and perhaps losing the advantage of surprise, so I put on walking gear, completely with a big, floppy hat, and set off across the fields.

After half a mile I turned on to a bridleway. It was the route Portia and Ophelia were most likely to use if they visited their friend, and always popular with riders, so I took to the side of a field with the hedge screening me from the path. Twice riders passed, and twice they failed to notice me at all, so when I heard a familiar, silvery laugh and the clip clop of hooves from ahead I simply ducked down behind an oak, listening and sure that they had no idea I was there for all the hammering of my heart. More laughter reached me, then Ophelia's voice, indistinct at first but quickly growing clear.

'... the look on her face, like she was sucking a turd! Then she let him fuck her tits!'

'Oh, she has huge tits, like a cow's udders or something.'

Again there was laughter, as the blood rushed to my face. It was obvious who they were talking about, me, and what I'd done with Mr Antrobus. The voice of the girl who'd made the remark about the size of my breasts wasn't familiar, too high for Portia or Ophelia and not quite so arrogant. It had to be Gemma. I risked a peep as they rode past, and sure enough, she was there, her flame red hair caught up in a pony-tail that bobbed to the motion of her horse. Ophelia was talking again, still on the same highly embarrassing topic.

'They are, and so heavy.'

'I'd love a feel. Do you think she'd let me whip them?'

'She'll do anything I say,' Portia added, 'and I do mean anything.'

'She really will,' Ophelia added, 'anything, and she'll love it. You should have seen her after we made her do the photographer guy. She was begging!'

'Did he fuck her?'

'No. She sucked him off, but when he came all the spunk came out around her lips ...'

'And out of her nose!'

'I thought she was going to puke!'

All three laughed, bringing my shame and anger up to boiling point, but I stayed down, knowing that I'd have little chance of imposing my will on all three of them at once, let alone while they were on horseback and in a country lane.

162

Gemma carried on.

'That would have been funny, but how did it go, afterwards?'

'Not too well,' Portia answered, suddenly serious. 'He was behaving like he owned the place.'

'Not after tomorrow,' Ophelia added. 'Not in …'

Her voice faded as they rode on, to leave me flushed and shaking, for what they'd said, for the way they talked about me, for the casual way they assumed I could be made Gemma's plaything, which was all the more embarrassing because it was true, or would have been but for Mr Antrobus. I was also puzzled by what they'd said at the end, because tomorrow was Sunday and they where supposed to be spying on me and James. That provoked a new and alarming thought, leaving me more determined than ever to get to the bottom of things.

As soon as they were out of sight I followed. They were presumably making for the Cedars. Gemma was on Marjorie's horse, which meant she'd be walking back alone, providing me with the ideal opportunity to waylay her, take her back to my house and spank her little round bottom for her. When she was done, then maybe she could have her wish and play with my breasts, only she wouldn't be whipping them. She'd be suckling on them before I put her on her knees to lick me to ecstasy.

It was only as I got close to the Cedars that I began to feel guilt and uncertainty. She deserved a spanking, but to accost her as she walked home alone came uncomfortably close to bullying, especially as she was so much younger than me. It would be better to confront all three of them, point out that what they'd done was unacceptable and offer atonement across my knee. I wouldn't suggest unpleasant alternatives, which would be blackmail, or threaten to do it by force, only ask for their submission to a just punishment.

For all the strength of my feelings it took courage to actually ring the doorbell. I was expecting Marjorie to answer it, which would have meant having to sit there sipping tea until I got a chance to speak to the girls alone, if I managed at all, but it was Ophelia who came to the door.

'Amber?' she said, surprised but with a touch of mockery in her voice as she went on. 'We were just talking about you. Portia, Gem, it's Amber!'

I followed her into the hall, a room in its own right, panelled in oak with further doors on two sides and a staircase curving up to a fine balcony on the fourth. There were signs of recent work, and dust sheets draped over what was presumably furniture beneath the stairs, but that did little to dilute the air of old-fashioned opulence, while the repairs looked as if they'd been done to the same high standards as the original. Evidently Marjorie was even more wealthy than I'd supposed.

'Excuse the mess,' Ophelia said casually. 'Workmen. Come into the drawing room.'

She led me through an open door, to a big, sunlit room, less grand than the hall and furnished for comfort but also in expensive good taste. Portia was seated in a huge armchair, Gemma on a sofa. Both looked up, Gemma a trifle uncertain but Portia with her usual cool, commanding smile.

'On your knees,' she ordered.

'No,' I responded, 'not now, Portia …'

'Don't worry,' she interrupted, 'my mother's gone into London and Gemma knows all about you. Now kneel.'

'No,' I repeated. 'I know Gemma knows all about me, and why, because Gemma hacked into my computer. You've been looking at my private pictures, haven't you? Don't deny it, because the photographer, Mr Antrobus, is an IT professional. He showed me exactly what you've done, and I know it was you.'

It was impossible to keep the blood from going to my face as I spoke, but Gemma's hand had gone to her mouth and Ophelia gave a nervous giggle, while even Portia's sounded as if I'd managed to dent her confidence as she answered me back.

'Does it matter?' she asked. 'We like to have you as our pet and you can't get enough of it, can you? Besides, we only did it to make sure we were right about you after Gem and I caught you playing with yourself in your car because those appalling travellers had spanked you.'

'That's as may be,' I answered her, 'but you shouldn't have done it, and while I don't want to lose what we've found together I do want to change things a little.'

'Fair enough,' Portia said. 'Let's have some time out to negotiate. What do you want, a promise that you get to come?'

'I want to spank you,' I told her, 'all three of you, regularly.'

'We only give,' she answered me, and then her pretty mouth had flickered up into the sadistic smile I knew so well, 'although, perhaps, I might allow you to punish Gemma.'

'Portia!' Gemma squeaked.

'Yes, punish Gemma,' Ophelia said ,'She's the one who hacked your computer, and she showed us the pictures. We wanted to play with you, that's all, and like Portia said, we don't take, we only give.'

'Since when!?' Gemma demanded.

There was a sudden silence.

'You get spanked?' I asked the girls.

'I said I only give,' Portia responded, and there was steel in her voice, but Ophelia had gone crimson.

They exchanged glances, Portia looking daggers at both Gemma and her sister as I struggled to work out the full implications of what had been said. I had Gemma, and if I played my cards right I had Ophelia too, even all three of them.

'So you do get spanked?' I said to Ophelia.

'You bitch!' she hissed, not at me, but at Gemma.

'You wanted me to get it!' Gemma retorted. 'And

165

anyway, you love it!'

'Who by?' I asked.

She had hung her head, looking down at the toe of her shoe, with which she was making little side to side motions of the carpet.

'Who do you think?' she said, her voice barely a whisper.

'Portia?' I asked. 'Gemma?'

'And then some ...,' Gemma began, only to be silenced by a sudden, harsh command from Portia.

'I want to explore my dominant side with Amber,' Ophelia went on sulkily. 'Now you've ruined it, Gemma. She won't fully respect me ...'

'No,' I told her. 'I'll have more respect for you. In fact, if you let me spank you I'll be even more compliant for you than I have been. There are some things I'll only let people do to me if I can switch with them, nice things.'

I'd been looking at Portia as I spoke, hoping she'd be tempted, but her expression didn't so much as twitch. Ophelia was still looking at the carpet, and spoke again, her voice as sulky as before.

'I don't see why I should get it anyway. I wasn't even there, the first time, with the travellers, and it's Gemma who hacked your computer. Spank her! Isn't that fair, Portia?'

Portia sat back in her chair, saying nothing, until the little motions Ophelia was making with her feet had grown so desperate I was wondering if she was going to wet herself. One thing was obvious. Whatever Portia said went, and at last she gave her verdict.

'Ophelia's right, it wouldn't be fair for you to spank her. You can spank Gemma.'

'Thank you, Miss Portia,' I responded, content to at least make a start on my revenge. 'Gemma, come here please.'

I'd sat down on a high backed chair as I spoke, and beckoned to Gemma. She got up, very slowly, glanced at the open door and for one moment I thought she was going to make a run for it, only for her to straighten up, swallow and address me.

'And if I let you, I can do the same to you?'

She bit her lip, still unsure, and glanced at Portia.

'Go on,' Portia ordered. 'You do deserve it.'

So did Portia, but this wasn't the time to point that out. I patted my lap, sure from what had been said that it wasn't her first time and hoping that a little show of authority would help her get over her misgivings. Her reaction was to glance at the door a second time, but then she was walking towards me, only to stop just a couple of feet away, her hands now folded in her lap. With her glasses on and her big, green eyes peering at me from beneath her fringe she looked deliciously vulnerable, adding to my delight and triumph for what I was about to do to her.

'Take off your jacket,' I told her.

'Are you going to make me strip?' she asked.

She'd given me permission, just by the way she said it, but I had other plans for her.

'Just do as you're told,' I said. 'Take off your jacket and open your blouse.'

'We make her strip,' Ophelia pointed out, no longer nervous now that it was her friend who got put through the pain and indignity of a punishment spanking.

Gemma didn't argue, but she was trembling as she shrugged off her smart black hunting jacket and began to undo her blouse. Her breasts were tiny, and she had no bra, so that as her blouse came open they were exposed, low, firm mounds of pale flesh topped by large, puffy nipples no darker than ordinary white skin. After taking a moment to admire them I reached up to push her blouse back, trapping her arms as I twisted my fist in the cotton, scruffing her so that I could pull her down across my knee. She went without resistance, just a little sob, and I noticed that she'd immediately gone up on her toes, lifting her bottom into classic spanking position.

'This is not your first time by a long way, is it?' I asked

167

as I pushed a thumb into the back of her jodhpurs. 'How often are you spanked.'

'Too often,' she answered, her voice soft, but with a trace of petulance.

'There's no such thing as too often for a girl like you,' I told her as I began to ease her jodhpurs down. 'You hacked into my computer, you stole pictures from my private collection and showed them to your friends, you took advantage of my sexuality. I think a little spanking is the least you deserve, don't you?'

'I suppose so,' she admitted as I settled her jodhpurs around her thighs.

'Yes, you do,' I went on, 'badly, and done properly, so we'd better pop these panties down, don't you think?'

This time she nodded, perhaps dumb with embarrassment but definitely just a little eager. She had on polka-dot panties, blue spots on white, quite full cut but rather too tight, so that they hugged every contour of her slim little cheeks.

'These suit you, Geekygirl,' I told her, 'so maybe …'

As I trailed off I tugged her panties tight up into the crease of her bottom, spilling out her sweet little cheeks and making her squeak in surprise and shock as the material was pulled hard between her legs, then again as I planted a smack across the meat of her bottom.

' …or maybe not,' I went on and I'd jerked her panties right down, exposing her bare bottom to the world, or at least to myself and to Portia and Ophelia, who were both watching in fascination.

Again Gemma reacted with a little squeak, repeated as I gave her a couple of firm slaps before pausing to inspect her bottom. She had extraordinarily pale skin, almost the white of thick cream, save for where she'd begun to pink up under my smacks, and just as smooth. Even her anus was white, a tight little pucker on full show between her slim cheeks, while the ginger hair and rosy flesh of her fanny made a gloriously rude contrast with the milk of the rest of her body.

'You're very pretty,' I told her. 'I bet the boys like to see you like this, from behind, and I bet you show them too, don't you?'

She didn't answer and I hadn't expected her to, so I took a fresh grip on the slack of her blouse between her shoulders and set to work on her bottom, slapping hard but with just the tips of my fingers to make it sting as much as possible. She reacted beautifully, yelping like a distressed puppy and kicking her long legs in her jodhpurs and panties, all of which encouraged me to spank harder.

I gave her fifty then stopped, allowing her to catch her breath and also to think it was over, when in fact I'd barely begun. It was just too satisfying to spank the girl who'd caused me to degrade myself so completely, while she was also too lovely to rush. Still holding her firmly in place I began to rub her now reddened bottom cheeks, my finger straying a little deeper with every touch, down towards her anus and the now puffy lips of her sex. Soon she'd begun to push her bottom up and I was already looking forward to taking my pleasure with her once her punishment was complete when Portia suddenly spoke up.

'On second thoughts,' she said, 'you can spank Ophelia too, but …'

'Portia!' Ophelia broke in. 'No!'

'Shut up,' her sister told her. 'I want to see you like that, over her knee while she touches you up, so yes, Amber, you can spank Ophelia, but there's a price.'

'Which is?' I asked, still stroking Gemma's bottom.

'Tomorrow,' she said, 'you have to ask James Sebastian to put you in a nappy.'

'A nappy!?' I echoed as Ophelia burst into giggles.

'A nappy,' Portia confirmed. 'A big white towel pinned up around your hips will do, as long as it's obvious you're in a nappy, for your spanking that is.'

'That's pretty kinky,' I pointed out. 'What if he doesn't want to do it?'

'Put one on anyway,' she said. 'In fact, you're to greet him like that.'

I hesitated, my spanking hand now resting lightly on Gemma's bottom as I considered my options.

'Remember, promise to do it and you can spank my sister,' Portia said.

I glanced at Ophelia, who was giggling behind her hand and plainly didn't expect me to accept Portia's offer.

'You can let him ride you while you're in your nappy,' she laughed. 'I want to see that!'

'I'll do it,' I said, 'if I can spank both of you.'

'That's the best way to get it yourself,' Portia answered. 'I do not take.'

Gemma made an odd little grunting noise and I realised that my fingers had strayed between her cheeks. I began to spank her again, somewhat absentmindedly. What Portia was suggesting was bitterly humiliating, but it was worth it.

'OK, I'll go in a nappy,' I said and had the pleasure of seeing Ophelia's mouth fall open in shock and dismay.

'Portia was only joking,' she said.

'No, I wasn't,' Portia answered her. 'It will be worth it.'

'You're not the one who's going to be spanked!' Ophelia protested. 'It's just not fair!'

For a moment I thought she was going to go for Portia, but she thought better of it and sat back, her face now set in a sulky pout as she watched me working on Gemma's bottom. Both little round cheeks were now flushed a rich pink, while her fanny had coloured up nicely and begun to juice in an inevitable response to her well-smacked bottom. I took hold of her long red hair, twisting it in my hand to pull her head back as I picked up the pace of her spanking. She started to kick and squirm again, wriggling her hot little bottom to show off her bumhole and cunt yet more blatantly than before, with the smacks of my hand on her flesh now punctuated by her cries.

I locked one leg around her calf, spreading her out and fixing her securely in position, then began to spank harder still, thinking of what she'd done as I laid into her bottom, indifferent to my now stinging hand for the pleasure of punishing her and to see her reaction. She was already out of control, but the harder my smacks got the more she struggled, now writhing on my lap with her legs kicking out and her bottom bucking up and down in her efforts to avoid the slaps, which only made her look more ridiculous. Her glasses fell off as she begun to toss her head up and down in her pain, and then she was thumping her fists on the carpet and begging me to stop, with her entire body writhing in my grip.

'All you have to do is say sorry,' I told her.

'Sorry!' she croaked, and I could hear the tears in her voice.

'Truly sorry?' I demanded.

'Yes! I'm sorry, I'm sorry, I'm sorry! I was only playing!'

'Thank you. A last few then.'

She'd burst into tears and my anger began to drain away immediately, but I wanted to spank her while she was crying, so that she'd know she had been properly punished, and because I knew what it would do to her. My hand was numb as I slapped at her cheeks, her legs were pumping and her bottom cheeks squeezing, the tight pink hole between opening and closing, then open wide as she let go a long, soft fart. At that I stopped and she immediately went limp, sobbing her heart out as she lay spanked and contrite across my legs, too well beaten even to bother to try and get up.

'There, you're done,' I told her, 'and you deserved that. Now give me a hug.'

I'd let go of her hair and opened my arms for her as she twisted around, coming willingly into my embrace, to apologise once more, then kiss me, her lips slightly parted as

171

they met mine. My hand found her bottom, cupping one burning cheek as I returned her kiss, and for a long moment our mouths were open together. I knew I could take it further, but contented myself with slipping one finger into the open wetness of her cunt before pulling her gently back.

'Not yet,' I told her. 'Now you can strip, naked, then into the corner you go, hands on your head and face to the wall so that you can think on your behaviour while we admire your smacked bottom. Go on.'

She went, peeling nude without complaint before scampering into the corner, where she pressed her nose and nipples to the wall and placed her hands on her head, her rosy bottom bare to the room. Even standing to attention as she did her corner-time, the lips of her fanny showed between her slim red cheeks, the hole now distinctly wet and a little open. Ophelia gave a nervous giggle for the sight.

'You needn't be so smug!' Gemma said. 'You're going to be the same in a minute, with your cunt showing to everybody.'

'Hush,' I told her. 'Right, Ophelia, come here.'

'I'm sorry,' Ophelia answered, her voice close to panic. 'I really am sorry, Amber, so you don't have to spank me quite so hard, do you? I mean it, and anyway, it was all Portia and Gemma, and I was always nice to you, wasn't I, and …'

'You peed all over me,' I pointed out.

'Just for fun!'

'Fair enough, I'll give you your spanking just for fun. Come here.'

She threw a nervous glance at Portia, who merely nodded in my direction, then rose to walk across to where I was seated. Just to take her hand was like an electric shock, and my heart was hammering as I tucked her into position across my knee with the taut seat of her jodhpurs towards her sister. Gemma had twisted around a little to watch but I didn't comment, happy to have both of them enjoy Ophelia's

172

spanking.

'Now then,' I told her. 'You and I have a bit of history together, don't we, Ophelia?'

'I suppose so,' she admitted.

'Spanking me, riding me, peeing on me, making me lick your bottom,' I went on, 'all very nice, I admit, but in my book that means you deserve the same. For now though, I'm going to content myself with taking down your jodhpurs, taking down your panties and spanking your little fat bottom until you howl!'

As I'd spoken I'd suited my actions to my words, hauling down first her jodhpurs and then the little white panties underneath to bare her bottom, across which I'd planted a single, hard smack. My hand still hurt from spanking Gemma so hard, but I wasn't going to let Ophelia get away with anything less and laid in from the start, reducing her to a squalling, kicking mess in just seconds. Like Gemma, she was so slim she showed everything behind, with her bumhole winking between her little cheeks and her bare pink fanny flaunted for her sister and her friend.

'Is that so funny?' I demanded as I spanked her, remembering how she always laughed at my own degradations. 'Is that so funny, now you're the one with a bare red bottom? No, it's not, is it, but it turns you on, doesn't it, just like it does to me, you little slut! Come on, let's have these legs apart so big sister gets a better view of your wet little cunt.'

She gave a gasp of shock as I hooked my leg around hers, just as I'd done to Gemma, spreading her wide to their gaze. As I went back to spanking her she was struggling, but only really instinctive jerks and wriggles to the pain of having her bottom slapped, making me all the more determined to get to her. Portia's whip was on the table and I snatched it up, drawing a highly satisfying squeal of pain and surprise from Ophelia as I lashed it down across her bottom.

'Be careful,' Portia warned.

I ignored her. She could do whatever she liked to me when I'd finished, but Ophelia was going to get the thrashing she deserved. It was working too, the whip leaving one scarlet line across her bottom after another as I beat her, while she was now struggling in earnest, kicking her feet up and down and tossing her long black hair in an agony of reaction to her punishment. She began to sob, but I continued, quite happy to reduce her to tears before I stopped, applying cut after cut to her squirming buttocks.

'Be careful,' Portia repeated, 'she sometimes … oh.'

She broke off as Ophelia let out a wail of shame and despair at the same instant a great gush of pee erupted from her cunt, all over my leg, into her panties and jodhpurs, all over the sofa, and all over the floor. I stopped immediately, but she couldn't, sobbing her heart out over my lap as the piddle bubbled from her open cunt, squirt after squirt in time to the pained contractions of her body. All I could do was hold on to her and let it come, sure that any change in position would only make a bigger mess and secretly enjoying the view and her shame as her urine ran down her belly and my leg.

'That's what I meant by be careful,' Portia remarked. 'If you beat her hard she tends to wet herself.'

'So I see,' I answered, still watching as Ophelia's stream died to a trickle. 'OK, darling, you can get up and give me a cuddle, then we'd better go and wash.'

'And you can clean up in here, Amber,' Portia added. 'In the nude, I think.'

'I just need that cuddle,' I told her. 'Come here, Gemma.'

I had to come, and while I was still in charge, for all that we obviously needed to clean up the puddle Ophelia had made. She'd done it all over my leg and I was going to have to take my lower clothes off at the very least, so I quickly pushed down my jeans and panties to spread my legs as Ophelia came into my arms. She was less contrite than Gemma, kissing me but also calling me a bitch, yet she was compliant enough, allowing me to ease her down to her knees as her friend came up beside her.

'Amber,' Portia said, but I ignored her, taking both girls by the hair and pulling them in between my open thighs.

'That's right,' I sighed as Ophelia's tongue touched my fanny. 'Lick me out … lick me out while you kneel in your own piss, Ophelia, and both of you with your little smacked bottoms all bare. Don't they look sweet, Portia? Doesn't this look right?'

She didn't answer, but she let me get on with it, my hands locked tight in the girls' hair as they licked me, Gemma now kissing at my hole while Ophelia worked on my clit. I pulled my legs up, offering them my open bottom and it was Ophelia who took the hint, immediately moving down to kiss my anus, then lick, probing at the little hole with the tip of her tongue as Gemma began to lick my fanny.

'That's right, lick my bottom, Ophelia,' I breathed, 'just like I lick yours, and your dirty sister's. You too, Gemma … go on, kiss my bumhole …'

I forced her head lower, twisting my fist in her beautiful red hair as I rubbed her nose between my bottom cheeks. She responded with a weak sob, trying to pull back, but then she'd done it, puckering up her pretty little mouth to kiss my anal ring and then sticking her tongue deep in up my hole. Ophelia began to work on my cunt once more and I closed my eyes in bliss, already starting to come.

My muscles began to contract, my legs squeezing on the girls' heads and my holes in contraction, juice squirting from my fanny as my anus went tight on Gemma's tongue. I was there, in ecstasy as they licked me, my mind running hot with thoughts of how they'd looked, spanked bare bottom across my lap, Gemma doing corner-time, Ophelia as she wet herself, how I'd made them cry and how they'd cuddled up to me, but best of all having them take turns to stick their tongues up my bottom while they licked me to orgasm.

Chapter Eleven

I got to help with the cleaning up, naked and on my knees as Portia had ordered, but I didn't care. For one thing I had both Gemma and Ophelia to help, also naked and crawling, but more importantly I'd spanked them both, as punishment, and received their submission in reward. That made all the difference in the world, and I even found myself taking a cynical amusement in the way Portia insisted on asserting her authority once we'd finished cleaning up, first riding me around the living room carpet, still nude, before sitting her bare bottom on my face to make me tongue her anus and lick her fanny until she'd come.

By then it was getting dangerous to be running around in the nude and we dressed again, not before time. Marjorie came back less than a quarter of an hour later and the girls went upstairs while she and I sipped tea in the drawing room, with me trying not to smile for my memories of what had been going on there earlier and she wrinkling her nose occasionally at the lingering aroma of her daughter's piddle and all four of our cunts.

I went home feeling thoroughly pleased with myself, although there was one small fly in the ointment, the price I'd agreed on in order to be able to spank Ophelia. Going in a nappy has to be about the most humiliating thing a grown woman can do, even with somebody who's heavily into it, and I had no reason to think James was. I couldn't back out either, because the girls were going to be watching and if I didn't play the game I knew I'd be unlikely to be allowed to dominate Ophelia again, while I was still determined on my ultimate goal, Portia herself.

From what had been said I knew that she got spanked, or at the very least had been spanked before, that the others knew and that she was desperate to keep it a secret from me. That meant it was possible, if only I could find the right conditions, and the excuse she needed in order to give in. Possibly it would be a bet or a challenge of some sort. Maybe she needed to feel that she had no choice, or was too drunk to stop it happening. Perhaps she simply needed to be alone with me. One way or another, I was convinced it was possible, because if somebody else had been invited to attend to her perfect little bottom, then so might I.

It was a thrilling thought, and also a comforting one as I laid out the biggest, fluffiest towel I could find on my bed the following morning. I'd bought two huge pins with pink plastic caps the night before, along with baby powder and a cream for nappy rash, all wicked little details the girls had added while Portia was queened on my face and Ophelia and Gemma were doing their best to get their own back for their spankings. Now I was going to have to put the awful thing on, and for James.

Just sitting my bottom down on the towel and pulling it up around my back and tummy was enough to put a huge lump in my throat, and as I clipped the pins into place at either hip I was biting my lip with raw chagrin. It actually felt rather nice, warm and snug around my bottom and belly, pleasantly tight at my hips and baggy between my legs, but a glance at myself in the mirror really brought home the humiliation of my situation.

It might only have been a towel, but there was no question that I looked the part, stark naked but for the huge, fluffy mass around my hips and over my bottom. I was in a nappy, a grown woman naked but for a nappy, my full breasts in ludicrous contrast to the white towelling around my hips. There was no possible way of hiding it either, which destroyed my plan of wearing it under my clothes and only revealing the state I was in to James once I had him nicely erect and too excited to worry about my perverted tastes. It was simply too big to hide.

I put a skirt on anyway, as trousers were out of the question, but that only made it worse, with the nappy bulging out beneath the hem so that it looked as if I'd been put in it because I was likely to wet myself. A top and boots made little difference, and I was red-faced and close to tears when I finally went downstairs to drink coffee in the kitchen, sitting on a chair with my bottom settled into the soft nappy material that bulged from between my thighs, as obscene as it was ridiculous.

Only thoughts of what I'd do to Portia kept me from running back upstairs as I waited for James, and when the bell finally went it took all my willpower to get up, let alone answer the door. I checked the spy-hole to make sure it was him, and that I wasn't about to open the door to some highly respectable neighbour and reveal myself in nappies. It was James, looking more debonair than ever in a smart but casual suit and holding a big bunch of flowers in one hand and a bottle of champagne in the other. I opened the door, grinning stupidly as his eyes swept me up and down.

'I ... I thought you might like it,' I said. 'To have ... to have me in nappies, for a spanking.'

He nodded, bemused but not unappreciative.

'I can't say it's something I've ever really considered,' he answered, his gaze once more moving to the bulge of towelling visible between my legs, 'but I must say you do look rather sweet.'

It was as good a reaction as I could possibly have expected and I found myself smiling in gratitude as I ushered him inside and hastily closed the door behind us.

'The champagne's already cold,' he said as we entered my kitchen, 'but before we have any, get out of those silly clothes. Girls who wear nappies don't need to worry about their modesty after all, do they?'

'No,' I admitted, more pleased than ever that he was making an effort to get into role, and as I started to strip my arousal had begun to balance my humiliation.

He watched, his handsome face full of amusement as I peeled, first topless, then down to nothing but my big, fluffy nappy.

'Very pretty,' he stated, 'now fetch a couple of glasses and you can come and sit on my knee.'

I obeyed, fetching a pair of champagne flutes and putting them out for us before settling my bottom onto his leg.

'I can see the pleasure in this,' he said as he pulled the foil on the champagne bottle loose, 'and I'm sure there could be a hundred and one reasons why you're going to need a spanking.'

He eased the cork free and filled our glasses, putting one hand to my bottom as he took a sip of the champagne. I followed suit, relaxing as he began to fondle me through the towelling of my nappy. There was still a big bubble of humiliation in my throat, but I knew that once I was turned on, and a little drunk, I'd be able to really enjoy the experience.

'Drinking for one thing,' he remarked, 'which definitely earns you a smacked bottom, and going about topless. Disgraceful behaviour!'

'You said girls in nappies didn't need to worry about their modesty!'

'With boobs like yours? You may not worry, but the boys will, this one anyway.'

He'd taken my hand and put it to his crotch so that I could feel his cock, already half stiff in his trousers. I gave him a squeeze and went back to my wine, determined not to rush things.

'I suppose I ought to be spanked then,' I admitted, 'outdoors perhaps, oh, and you were going to ride me.'

'Isn't that rather mixing our fetishes?' he questioned.

179

'But I shall certainly spank you anyway, here and now.'

He'd taken the glass from my hand even as he spoke, and the next moment I'd been upended across one leg, the other trapping my thighs. Once again his hand found my bottom, to squeeze my cheeks through my nappy before applying a firm smack, which I could hardly feel.

'Ow,' I said, doing my best to sound sarcastic. 'Try harder.'

'It is a problem, yes,' he admitted. 'Do I pull your nappy down and spoil the effect of you having it on, or do I smack your legs?'

'Hey, no! Ow!' I squeaked as he suited action to word, releasing a volley of stinging smacks to the back of my bare thighs. 'That's not fair!'

He merely laughed and gave me a few more smacks before once more beginning to fondle my bottom through my nappy. It felt nice, and the pain of having my legs slapped had got to me, so I lifted my hips in invitation. His hand slid in under my nappy, to feel my bare skin, on my cheeks and then between, tickling my anus and the lips of my fanny before sticking one long finger in up my hole.

'You're already wet,' he pointed out as he inserted a second digit.

'I know. I can't help it.'

I let myself go limp, enjoying being fingered and the delicious shame of my position. Already the wine had begun to go to my head a little, and I was getting horny enough to fully explore the fantasy, but part of that was to let the girls watch.

'Take me outdoors,' I begged. 'I want to be more exposed.'

'You're a disgrace,' he answered me, but his fingers had pulled from my fanny and after applying a few more firm slaps to the backs of my thighs he let me up.

We downed what was left of the champagne and I was led outside by the hand, into the paddock, where he seated himself on the double bar of a jump and put me back over his knee for more spanking. Again it was on my thighs, a painful part of being in nappies I hadn't foreseen, but after a while he decided on a new technique, pulling the towelling to one side to bare half my bottom, then the other, allowing him to spank each cheek in turn. I was soon hot and hornier than ever, ready for whatever he wanted to do and looking forward to being thoroughly humiliated in front of the girls, but there was no sign of them.

'Time to ride me,' I said when he finally let me down from his lap, for all that his hand had gone to his fly.

'If you insist,' he said, 'although, um …'

He squeezed his cock as he spoke, showing off the full erection hidden by his trousers, purely from spanking my nappy-clad bottom. I ran for my workroom, determined to give Portia everything she had demanded, because although there was no sign of the girls I was sure they'd be watching. Grabbing my harness, I rushed back, to find James still sitting on the jump, but with his cock and balls out of his trousers. He grinned as I approached.

'Maybe it's the sight of you in that nappy,' he said, 'or maybe it's because I've been saving myself for you all week, but I need you to suck me now. After that I'll take you for a ride.'

I nodded and got down on my knees to take his big, pale cock in my mouth. The last man I'd sucked had been Mr Antrobus, and it felt wonderful to have a good-sized erection in my mouth again, and to be sucking a man I really liked. His hand settled on my head as I got to work, stroking my hair and the nape of my neck as I licked and kissed at his penis. Soon his other hand had gone to the shaft of his cock, masturbating into my mouth with rising urgency. I took hold of my boobs, squeezing them to show off for him and stimulate myself, and as my own pleasure rose I'd stuck a hand down the front of my nappy.

My fanny was warm and wet, open from when he'd

181

fingered me and badly in need of my touch, as was my bottom, both cheeks hot inside the material of my nappy. I began to explore myself as I sucked on his cock, enjoying both the feel of my naked flesh and the towelling that encased my hips and belly and bottom. A sudden urge came over me, to wet myself as I sucked on his cock, and before I could think twice I'd let go. My hand was under my cunt, cupping the soft, warm mound as my pee erupted into my fingers, splashing out to trickle down my thighs and soak into my nappy.

It felt wonderful, far too good to hold back, and I let go completely, crying out around my mouthful of cock as I filled my nappy. James realised what I'd done and swore under his breath, calling me a filthy tart as his grip tightened in my hair and the motion of his hand on his shaft grew faster, his fist smacking into my lips as I struggled to keep sucking as spurt after spurt of piddle erupted into my nappy. He was going to come, the sight of me soiling my nappy too much to let him hold back, and with a final hard tug at his cock he had. I felt the spunk erupt down my throat, and more, over my nose and in one eye as he jerked my head back to wank off in my face. A third spurt caught me across one cheek and in my open mouth, another hit my chin and splashed my boobs before he gripped hard on his cock to squeeze out what was left onto the very tip of my nose.

At last he let go of my hair, but I stayed as I was, squatting on the ground with the piddle still running from my open cunt and the spunk slithering slowly down my face. I began to masturbate again, utterly shameless in front of him, with my sodden nappy now bagging heavy under my bottom. Another moment and I was there, crying out in ecstasy as every filthy detail of what we'd done came together in my head, my spanked bottom, my spunk-soiled face, but best of all the soggy nappy now hanging low on my hips from the weight of what I'd done in it.

Finally I came down, my head hung in exhaustion and

also shame as I knelt in front of my lover, soiled and filthy, but also blissfully happy, just so long as I had his approval. When I finally found the courage to look up he was smiling, and then reached out to pat my head as if I were a pet dog, badly behaved but too loyal and endearing to be angry with. I returned his smile as I sat back, only to lose my balance and sit down in my soggy nappy.

'I'd better clean up!' I told him.

'Oh no you don't,' he laughed. 'I'm going to take you for a ride, just like that, so you can think on what a dirty girl you've been for a while. Saddle up.'

I nodded eagerly, glad that he was still keen to play after he'd come, unlike the vast majority of men I've met. Picking up my saddle, I quickly buckled the girth strap into place around my tummy and adjusted the stirrups for his long legs. He watched in approval as I added my bridle, with the bit held between my teeth as I adjusted the straps to encase my head in a tight leather cage with the reins hanging down my back. My pads followed and I was ready, a crawling pony-girl once again, although he was right about the nappy, which had been fun but no longer suited our game and was starting to feel uncomfortable.

'I think I'd better hose you down,' he said, 'but I'll ride you into the yard.'

He climbed onto my back, cautiously, allowing his weight to settle onto me only very slowly. I knew I could take it, and more, but appreciated his care, giving a toss of my hair in thanks before I set off, crawling towards the arch, through which Marjorie Crowthorne-Jones had just emerged.

I stopped, caught, too taken aback to move. There could be no talking my way out of it, no explanation save the awful truth. Naked outdoors with a man would have been bad enough, a fine piece of gossip for the neighbourhood. Naked and in harness would have been far worse, kinky as well as rude. Naked but for a nappy would have been worse still, enough to excite not only condemnation but pitying remarks about my need for a psychotherapist. Naked, saddled up with a man riding on my back, and wearing not merely a nappy but a deliberately used nappy took the outrage I was committing to a whole new level, far beyond anything a woman like Marjorie could be expected to cope with. She screamed.

With that, everything began to happen at once. Marjorie ran back through the arch, closely followed by James, who was babbling something about being able to explain. I heard the sound of laughter, faint but silvery and quite unmistakable, and as I turned I caught a glimpse of Ophelia's face among the bushes, twisted in shock and delight, like some demented imp. A glimpse of red hair deeper in among the leaves showed that she wasn't the only one watching. Then Portia appeared, further down the banks, gave a shrug which might have been commiseration, even apology, for all that her face was glowing with triumph, and ran. Ophelia followed, linked hands with her sister as they reached the Old Sidings, with Gemma racing to catch up, and they were gone.

I stayed where I was, unable to follow the girls as I could hardly chase them down the road in my nappy and harness, and not wanting to go into the yard, where James and Marjorie were having a furious argument. It was also very telling, with Marjorie accusing James of being a pervert, and more importantly, of being unfaithful. That was really all I needed to know, but as I listened the situation became slowly and painfully clear, in detail.

They were in a relationship, or rather, they had been, as she was making it abundantly clear that this was no longer the case. She also found his love of spanking peculiar, as she could only see it as punishment, which explained why he had found it hard to take in when I'd claimed that she punished me for pleasure. His response was that if she wasn't willing to give him what he needed then she shouldn't be surprised if he found somebody who would, which didn't go down well at all, although he made a point of denying responsibility for either the harness or the nappy. Both of those, he made clear, had been my idea.

On hearing that I finally found the nerve to step forward, my anger overcoming the blazing embarrassment which had held me rooted to the spot. At the very least I felt he might have defended me, when I had given myself to him so completely, but his only concern seemed to be to save his own skin. My hands had gone to the first of my nappy pins, but I hesitated, realising that if I took it off I would only make a bigger exhibition of myself than I already had. I paused to unbuckled my harness instead, but as I struggled to get the straps open the argument stopped.

I tugged off my saddle and pulled the bit out of my mouth as I hurried forward, determined to confront James, but when I reached the yard he was gone. Marjorie was still there, silent and tense, her face set in frozen distaste. I had to say something, and it was far too late for denials, but I could at least try and make it plain that I hadn't been aware of the full truth.

'I didn't know,' I said, 'about you and James.'

She answered with icy reserve.

'Pray do not concern yourself.'

'And I'm sorry if we shocked you,' I went on, my voice no less formal, 'but what I choose to do in the privacy of my own home is really nothing to do with you.'

'I am not concerned with your ... your peculiar and frankly disgusting behaviour,' she answered me, 'only that you chose to indulge yourself with a man ...'

'Who is obviously completely unsuitable for you,' I interrupted, 'and not just because he enjoys the sort of thing we were doing, but because he could never be faithful to anybody. Isn't it just as well you found out now?'

'That is true,' she admitted, the hurt now showing in her voice, 'but you must have known?'

'No,' I insisted. 'You didn't mention him, and I've never seen the two of you together, have I? He must have known the risks though, and he obviously didn't care.'

'That is also true,' she said thoughtfully, 'as had you not been unwell the other day you would have met him at my garden party.'

'Yes ...,' I began, and then realised the implications of what she'd said. 'Who said I was unwell?'

'Portia.'

'I wasn't unwell. She ... she didn't want me to come. Now I see why.'

'I don't understand you.'

'Why did you come over this morning?'

'Portia suggested ...'

'I bet she did!'

'Are you implying that Portia is in some way responsible for all this?'

'Yes,' I answered as the awful suspicion that had been growing in my mind became certainty. 'I am. She introduced me to James Sebastian. She knows we've been seeing each other, but I don't suppose she told you, did she? She ...'

I stopped, unwilling to admit that it was also Portia who'd made sure that James and I weren't merely together but doing something so outrageous that there could be no possible way he would be able to talk himself out of the situation. It wasn't necessary. Marjorie's expression had grown colder still and her face had gone dark as the truth sank in.

'I don't suppose Portia and Ophelia wanted you and James to be together?' I suggested.

'No,' she answered. 'They did not. Excuse me, Miss Oakley.'

When Marjorie had gone I went indoors to clean up. I was furious, with James, with Ophelia, but most of all with

186

Portia. She had quite obviously set the whole thing up, manipulating me in order to break up her mother's relationship. I could see why she had done it, because it was more than likely that James intention had been to marry Marjorie, ensure a speedy divorce and walk away with a chunk of what had to be a sizeable fortune, but that in no way excused her behaviour, nor getting her kicks out of me along the way.

I'd wanted to spank her before, but now I wanted to strangle her. When I thought of all the indignities she'd inflicted on me, and how much I'd enjoyed them, it made me choke with fury, while making sure her mother caught me saddled up and in a nappy was the final insult. By the time I'd washed and dressed I was beyond caring for the consequences of my actions. I had to confront her, and marched over to the Cedars in a state of fury so strong that when nobody answered the doorbell I went straight to the drawing room window, intending to rap on the glass.

What I saw stopped me with my fist raised to the glass. Portia lay across her mother's lap, her black skinny jeans around her knees, her panties pulled down, her little round bottom red with spanking. She was in tears, her pretty face screwed up in utter misery, while the big mirror on the opposite wall reflected not only her smacked bottom but the sweetly turned cunt and tight pink anus I had enjoyed licking so well. Now I knew who spanked Portia Crowthorne-Jones, her mother, and not only Portia. Ophelia sat to one side, looking no less miserable than her sister as she watched the spanking, and while she had her skirt on the little white panties tangled around her ankles made it very clear that she had received the same treatment. More astonishing still was Gemma, standing by the sofa with a pair of polka-dot panties rolled down to the level of her knees and her skirt held up to show off the triangle of ginger fur between her thighs, her face working with apprehension as she waited her turn.

I moved away from the window, my anger gone, to be replaced by confusion and doubt for everything I held dear. Portia wasn't fighting, so had presumably accepted her spanking as just, yet she was being punished and there was nothing remotely erotic about the situation, not for her, nor for Marjorie, nor for Ophelia, although in Gemma's case I wasn't quite so sure, or why else accept a punishment from a friend's mother? There was no doubt about my own reaction though, an instant flush of satisfaction to see her getting what she so richly deserved immediately followed by a near unbearable mixture of guilt and arousal.

Not to look again would have been impossible. Cautious this time, I peeped in at the window, just in time to catch the end of Portia's spanking, a dozen or more furious swats to her dancing cheeks that set her howling like a baby before she was let up to join her sister. She left her jeans and panties down, fiddling nervously with the hem of her blouse as the tears streamed down her face, but she was watching as Marjorie beckoned to Gemma. There was no resistance, just a single, sulky look for the woman about to spank her as Gemma laid herself down across Marjorie's lap, little white bottom high so that, as with Portia, her cunt and anus showed in the mirror.

As Gemma's spanking began I had moved away again, but I knew what I wanted to do, a crazy, irrational desire that I simply could not resist. Moving like a clockwork toy I stepped back to the front door and twisted the handle. It wasn't locked and I went in, across the hall to the open drawing-room door, beyond which I could hear the smacks of Marjorie's hand on Gemma's bare bottom, along with cries of pain and Portia's gentle snivelling. They didn't notice me for a moment, Marjorie too busy with the task at hand and the girls staring in fascination at their friend's bouncing bottom cheeks, and I had to speak up to draw their attention.

'If you're going to do that to them,' I told Marjorie, 'you

had better do the same to me.'

She looked around, doubtful, surprised, then suddenly stern once more.

'Very well. Pull up your skirt and take down your pants.'

I obeyed, with Portia and Ophelia staring at me in amazement as I rolled my panties down to my knees and lifted my skirt to show myself off back and front, just as Gemma had done to await the spanking she was now getting. She'd seen me too, but she didn't seem to care, too worried for the hard smacks being applied to her bare bottom, and Marjorie definitely knew how to spank. Gemma's bottom was already rosy all over, but I knew the spanking would be long and firm, a proper punishment, and exactly what I'd needed all my life.

When my turn finally came I was shaking like a jelly, but I was as good as the others, laying myself across Marjorie's lap with my bottom lifted. There was no preamble, no gentle, warming pats, just a firm, purposeful spanking from the very first slap as she told me off for my bad behaviour. I was in tears from the start, no better than Portia, crying my eyes out as smack after smack landed across my bottom. She obviously didn't care that I was older than the others, or that I hadn't known about her and James, dishing out the same firm, well deserved spanking to my naked bottom cheeks to leave me squealing like a pig and blubbering out apologies, every bit as miserable and contrite as the three girls who were watching me as they sat on their hot bottoms with their panties around their legs.

I came, a beautiful, perfect orgasm just from the sensation of being spanked so well, but my cry of ecstasy was lost among my sobs and gasps of pain. If Marjorie noticed what had happened her sole response was to spank harder still, to set me howling my head off and thrashing crazily across her lap, but when it finally stopped and I was permitted to get up I caught Portia's eye, to share a glance as knowing as it was filled with shame.

'Leave your pants down,' Marjorie instructed, 'and get out of my sight, all of you.'

We ran from the room. I could have left, but I knew full well what was about to happen and followed the other upstairs in a procession of contrite, well-spanked girls, our panties clutched in our fists and our bare red bottoms bobbing behind us. Portia was in front and we followed her up one flight of stairs and a second, then a steep spiral of cast-iron steps to a big, open attic room, empty but for three huge bean bags, some old chairs and a scattering of cushions arranged around an entertainment centre.

Ophelia was in Portia's arms immediately, and it was left to me to lower the trapdoor into place before cuddling up to an eager, wriggling Gemma. Her fingers had pushed up into my cunt even as I cupped her hot little bottom and our mouths came open together as we began to kiss. Whether Marjorie suspected what was going on, and obviously had been going on for ages, I neither knew nor cared. All I wanted was what the girls had to give, consolation for our pain and humiliation, along with relief for the heat our spankings had brought to our cunts.

We stayed in our pairs, Portia and Ophelia sharing one bean bag, Gemma and I another as we kissed and licked and caressed each others' bodies with rising urgency. When Gemma went down to kiss my fanny I twisted her slight body around to return the favour, pulling her on top of me with her thighs spread in my face and my mouth to her cunt. My hands found her bottom cheeks, still hot from her spanking, and I spread them wide to stretch out her anus, remembering how I'd promised to lick her bottom.

I did it immediately, sticking my tongue out to lap at the tiny white star and make her sigh with pleasure before returning my attention to her cunt. Besides us, Portia and Ophelia were locked in the same rude embrace, each with her face buried between the other's thighs as she licked busily at the folds and crevices of her sister's cunt. I heard

Ophelia's cry of ecstasy and I knew she'd come, with Gemma not far behind, Portia and myself last, our cries of ecstasy mingled as tongues and fingers worked on our clits. We broke apart, gasping for breath, Ophelia now giggling, Gemma immediately rolling on her face to reach back and squeeze her smacked cheeks.

'That hurt!' she complained. 'Your mother spanks so hard!'

'You knew what was coming,' Portia told her, 'but we did it, didn't we!? No more James Sebastian, thanks to Amber!'

'Yes, thanks to Amber,' I said, 'and yes, your mother does spank hard, and yes, I was in a nappy and my harness when she caught us, so …'

'A dirty nappy!' Ophelia laughed.

'Yes,' I admitted, 'a dirty nappy, so perhaps, Portia, you owe me something?'

She was silent for a moment before she answered.

'I'm sorry.'

'A little more?' I urged.

'I'm truly sorry,' she answered, 'but please understand that we had to find somebody he couldn't resist. We knew he was into sexy spanking because Ophelia heard him trying to talk Mum into it, so when we found out about you, well, we had to try, and we couldn't really explain, could we?'

'No,' I admitted, 'but that wasn't what I had in mind when I said a little more.'

I'd stood up as she was talking, and now extended my hand to her. She'd kicked off her lower garments while she was in a tangle with her sister and was nude from the waist down, an enticing sight with the hair of her fanny making a tight V between her thighs, but the wrong way up for my purposes.

'Come on,' I told her, my hand still extended, 'it's not going to be hard, but I think we both know it needs to be done.'

Her expression had changed as the implication of what I was saying sank in, from satisfaction to shock, but she took my hand. I lifted her, very gently, holding her by the hand as I led her across to one of the old chairs.

'She's going to spank her,' Ophelia whispered, and Portia nodded, the final acceptance of my right to deal with her bottom.

Her resistance was gone, her head hung down as I took my seat, and she went across my knee without having to be told. I'd promised it wouldn't be hard and I meant it, because I didn't need to hurt her. What I needed was her freely offered bottom, bare and raised to show off her pretty cunt and the tight pink star of her anus, her modesty completely surrendered as she gave herself up for spanking. A single pat would have done it, but when I'd given her half a dozen and stopped she made no effort to rise.

I carried on, scarcely able to take in that I had her over my knee for a spanking and without the slightest resistance. After a while I paused to unbutton her blouse and pull up the little white bra beneath, exposing her breasts before once more starting to spank her. Still she stayed put, her breathing deep and even, just as compliant as any other girl I'd had across my knee. I pulled off her blouse and bra, leaving her naked, and when I began to spank again I was using proper, open-handed slaps. She began to gasp and whimper, but still made no attempt to get up, for all that her mother had turned her bottom a rich red before I'd even got to work on her.

'Spank me properly,' she gasped. 'Go on, punish me.'

'I will,' I told her, 'and you do deserve this, Portia.'

As I spoke I'd tightened my grip on her waist and began to spank harder still, bringing my hand down across the crest of her cheeks with all my force, again and again, as hard as I'd ever spanked anybody. She began to kick and struggle in my grip, but as I eased off she spoke again.

'Don't stop ... spank me, spank me hard, Amber. Really punish me!'

Her voice broke to a choking sob as she finished and I realised she was crying, just as she had been over her mother's knee, and just as I did whenever I was properly taken to task. I knew how she felt, and what to do, bringing the smacks up to full force again until she was writhing and kicking, with her cunt spread to the room, her long hair tossing up and down and her fists beating on the floor, sobbing her heart out with the tears spraying from her eyes and she gave in completely to the pain of her spanking.

I didn't want to stop any more, and she didn't want me to either, lost to her feelings but making no effort whatsoever to get up, nor asking for the spanking to end. Yet it had to eventually, and we both knew there was going to be a next time, so I finally stopped and hauled her up to take her into my arms. She immediately cuddled on to me, clinging tight and shaking, with the tears still streaming down her face. I held her tight, and when her sobs at last began to die down I pushed a hand between our bodies to pull up my top and lift one breast from my bra.

She understood what I was offering and accepted without hesitation, letting me cradle her in my arms and feed my nipple into her mouth to let her suckle on me. As she fed I began to stroke her hair and the nape of her neck, giving her what she needed and pointedly ignoring her giggling sister and Gemma, who just seemed awestruck to see a spanked girl put to suckle the woman who'd punished her, never mind that it was Portia.

I let her take her time, holding her to my chest until she chose to release my nipple from her mouth. We both knew what came next, and I had let my thighs come open even as she went to her knees. Her tongue found my clitoris and she'd begun to lick. I could have come like that, so easily, but there was one thing more to be done. Taking her gently by the hair, I allowed my body to slide forward a little.

'And my bottom hole,' I told her.

There was a moment of resistance, no more, before she

had gone down, to spread my bottom with her thumbs and plant a single, firm kiss on my anus. I'd have let her get away with that, but she began to lick, her tongue flicking on the sensitive skin around my bumhole and in, pushing right up to make me sigh in ecstasy and send both Ophelia and Gemma into fits of giggles as they realised that Portia was licking my bottom.

'What's so funny?' I demanded, desperately trying to sound stern. 'You're no better. Come on, help her.'

Both crawled over and I let my thighs go as wide as they could as the three girls crowded between, to lick and kiss at my thighs and the tuck of my bottom, at my fanny and bumhole, their tongues lapping and probing at me until at last it was too much and I came, screaming out in ecstasy as my climax tore through me, so hard and so long that I came close to blacking out, and at the supreme moment the image in my mind was of Portia, so beautiful, so dominant, now stark naked between my open thighs with her spanked bottom thrust out behind her and her tongue as deep up my bottom hole as she could manage.

Chapter Twelve

Two weeks later Kay came home. Things had calmed down a little by then, but the situation still took a little bit of explaining. Not that she minded the girls, as she was always ready to accept new female playmates, but she felt I'd gone too far with James. I accepted six hard strokes of the cane, naked and touching my toes in the workroom, which made me feel a lot better, but she was also upset about Hannah and that was less easy to resolve. She has always had more of a social conscience than me, and felt that I should have put my friends first. Yet there was nothing to be done about it, or so I thought.

When she'd been back a week she suggested we walk up through Pembridge Woods to look for early porcini mushrooms. It seemed a good idea and we set off under blue skies and along sun-dappled paths, holding hands and both in high spirits. She was sure she knew a good spot for mushrooms on the far side of the woods, but as we approached I caught the scent of bacon on the air, which seemed odd in the middle of the countryside. There was also a dun-coloured goat browsing beside the track, which I was sure I'd seen somewhere before.

'That's strange,' I said, sniffing, then saw that Kay was looking at me with the same determined expression she always wore when she wanted to turn the tables and give me a spanking. 'Oh, you haven't, have you?'

'Hannah called,' she said. 'No, let's have the truth. I called Hannah. She wants to punish you, so if you'd rather she didn't we should turn back now.'

We'd reached a turn in the path, where it grew wider before leaving the woods. Two familiar caravans were parked to one side, at right angles to each other and an equally familiar truck, creating a square space blocked from the sight of the path. I stopped, half wanting to run, half to stay and take what was coming to me. Kay gave me an encouraging smile and I'd decided.

'No mushrooms then?' I asked.

'I think you might find one or two,' she said and Leary and Sean emerged between the caravans, 'but they might not be as tasty as porcini.'

'Very funny,' I responded. 'You're going to get it for this, Kay, but all right, I suppose it's only fair. Come on, boys, I'm all yours.'

They closed in on me, grinning. Both knew the score, Leary immediately pulling up my top to take my breasts in his big hands, weighing them as if they'd been a pair of melons. He gave a grunt of appreciation, his dirty fingers soiling my bra as he groped, while Sean had gone behind me to take a handful of my bottom. I put my hands on my head, already shaking as they molested me but knowing I'd be all right once my feelings kicked in.

'Behind the caravan, you idiots,' Hannah chided as she appeared from the same gap the men had used. 'This is a public footpath. You know, Kay, I didn't think she'd come. So she's going to take it, whatever we dish out?'

'Yes,' I told her as Leary and Sean began to hustle me across to the caravans. 'I'm sorry, Hannah.'

'You will be,' she assured me. 'Cup of tea, Kay?'

'Yes, please,' Kay answered. 'You're not going to be too rough with her, are you?'

'Nothing she can't handle,' Hannah answered. 'Maggie, she's here, put the kettle on, and pass out the margarine. Right, slut, on your knees and get sucking.'

We'd reached the square made by the three vehicles and

the dense foliage at the edge of the wood, an area quite private enough for my punishment but also very much exposed. I'd had it anyway, and let myself be pushed down into a kneeling position on the dirty ground beside the brazier on which they'd been cooking a late breakfast. My bra was pulled up and big, grubby hands found my breasts as they came naked, both of them groping happily until Sean let go in order to pull his cock out, a long, skinny thing as pale and ugly as he was and hanging over a pair of fat little balls densely grown with rust-coloured hair. I hesitated and had my cheeks squeezed for my pains, to force me to open my mouth and take him in, sucking as Leary in turn freed his penis. He was bigger than Sean, or at least fatter, if not so long, a bulky cock on bulky balls and a lot more desirable than his friend. I swapped, taking Sean in my hand as I sucked on Leary's cock, with both already beginning to stiffen.

'Willing little tart, ain't she,' Hannah remarked as she accepted a tub of cheap margarine from Maggie. 'Fetch the block.'

I glanced to the side to see what they were doing and my heart began to beat faster as I saw that Maggie had lifted a squat wooden frame with a cushion on top of it, obviously a home-made whipping block and equally obviously what I was to be bent over, maybe for fucking, maybe to be beaten, most likely both.

'Get over it,' Maggie ordered as she put it down beside where I was working on the men's cocks. 'Arse up, legs spread.'

The men were already hauling me towards the whipping block, Leary with his cock still in my mouth. I was spread out on it, my thighs pulled apart and rough twine wound around my legs and arms, Maggie and Sean working to tie me securely in place as Leary continued to use my mouth. By the time I was properly bound and helpless he was erect, and Sean took his place to leave him to pull down my jeans and panties, stripping me bare behind without ceremony. I thought he'd spank me, but he came around to the side to rub the head of his cock on my flesh where one boob was squashed out on the block.

'Nice boobs,' he remarked, 'big. Shame we can't fuck 'em.'

'You get to fuck better than that,' Hannah assured him. 'I want her buggered.'

'Oh yeah, right up that big fat arse!' Sean crowed as he began to masturbate into my mouth.

'Count on us for a buggering,' Leary agreed,

A shock of fear and consternation had hit me for my fate, but there was nothing I could do, tied and helpless with two men now erect and ready for the little hole between my cheeks, neither likely to take no for an answer if I protested, while I had told Hannah I'd take her punishment.

'You'll have to lube her up,' Kay pointed out.

'We know,' Maggie pointed out. 'What do you think the marge is for?'

'Oh, I see,' Kay replied. 'Pass me the tub then, I'd better do it.'

I stuck up my bottom, resigned to my fate and still sucking on Sean's helmet as he wanked into my mouth, now with his trousers and underpants halfway down around his hips. I was hoping he'd spunk and save me at least one cock up my bottom, but I was definitely going to get one, because Leary was already behind me, nursing his erection to keep it nicely stiff for my hole. I could see he was keen too, his face set in fascination as he watched Kay smear margarine between the cheeks of my bottom, and when she pushed a finger in up my anus his tongue flicked out to moisten his lips in anticipation.

It was impossible not to respond, with my girlfriend's finger up my bottom and a long, stiff cock in my mouth. Maggie laughed to hear my sigh and Kay gave me a friendly slap across one bare cheek, at which Hannah spoke.

'No spanking, she likes it too much. Just get her ready, then fuck her arse.'

'Yes, Hannah,' Kay answered and eased another finger into my bottom hole.

I couldn't help but react, wide-eyed and gulping on Sean's cock as she worked my anus open, pushing her fingers in and out, then spreading them to allow a third inside. Already my hole felt loose enough for a cock, which was just as well, because Leary's erection was impressively thick and as wide at the base as any I'd ever seen. Men always boast about how long their cocks are, but for a woman it's the width that matters, especially when she's being buggered.

'Are you ready there?' Sean demanded. 'Cause I swear if you're not I'll do it in her mouth.'

'Stop wanking in it then,' Kay advised, and she'd slipped her last two digits in up my gaping bottom hole. 'I'm going to fist her to make sure she's really ready.'

I tried to pull back so I could tell her it wasn't necessary, but Sean chose that moment to force his cock down my throat, just as Kay's knuckles pushed in up my straining hole, making me choke. Suddenly my mouth was full of spunk as he came despite himself, grunting as he tossed at his shaft, then abruptly jamming it deep into my gullet. The muscles of my throat went into violent contraction, spunk exploded from my nose and out around his cock shaft, then worse as I threw up all over his cock and balls and into his half lowered trousers and underpants.

'You daft bitch!' he swore, but the others were laughing and he was forced to make an ignominious retreat.

'Are you all right?' Kay asked and I managed a weak nod, knowing that the best I could hope for was a bucket of water in my face to wash off the mixture of spunk and sick dribbling down my chin. I would get buggered anyway.

I got the bucket of water, icy cold and delivered by Maggie from a few inches, to leave me gasping and shaking my head.

'She's got to be ready, surely?' Maggie asked Kay as she emptied what remained in the bucket over my head.

'I suppose so,' Kay admitted, 'but I don't often get to fist her, especially up her bum, and she often does it to me. Both holes at once sometimes.'

'Is that right?' Leary asked. 'Well anytime you need a portion of good Irish beef, just you call me. Now come on with you.'

'Oh all right,' Kay answered.

Her entire hand was up my bottom, all the way to her wrist, and as she pulled it out I was left gulping in air and shaking my head in reaction. I'd never felt so open behind, my anus wide and slack, so that I pictured my hole as a gaping pink tunnel more than capable of accommodating even Leary's cock.

I was about to find out, as he got behind me, wanking furiously at his shaft with one hand on my spread bottom. My hole had begun to close, but not for long as he pressed his helmet between my cheeks, wiping it in the slit of my bottom then pressing it to my anus. I felt my slimy hole start to open once more, stretching easily to accommodate first his helmet and then the thick, gnarled bulk of his shaft, pushed slowly up, inch by inch, until at last he was all the way in, with his balls pressed firmly to my empty cunt.

'Now that's what I like to see,' Hannah remarked, 'a well buggered tart. Come over on my lap, Kay.'

She went, sitting down on Hannah's broad lap as Leary begun to fuck my anus, pumping his cock in the slippery cavity to set me panting and clutching as the legs of the whipping block. He felt huge, as if his cock was going to push right through me and out of my mouth as he buggered me, while with every push his heavy scrotum slapped against my fanny, only just too high to get me off. It drove me crazy, wriggling in my bonds and begging him to fuck me harder in the hope that he'd get me there, and wishing I

200

could have got a hand to my cunt.

I thought it would happen, his thrusts growing deeper and faster, ramming into me to squash out the meat of my bottom and jam his balls to my sex, again and again, until at last I felt my muscles start to contract, at which he stopped, grunting as he held himself deep to fill my rectum with spunk. He'd come, and immediately pulled out, leaving me sobbing with frustration as my well buggered hole closed with a soft fart.

'Put it in her mouth,' Hannah ordered, and as Leary's spunk began to dribble from my bottom hole I was being presented with the fat cock he'd just had in my rectum.

'Such a slut,' Maggie remarked as I began to suck on Leary's dirty cock, lost to even the faintest sense of decency. 'Will you just look at her, sucking on a prick that's been up her arse and happy to do it!'

'She'll not handle the next one so easily,' Hannah replied. 'Bring Rathwell.'

'Morris?' I said weakly as Leary withdrew from my mouth.

Hannah just laughed and I realised what she meant. I let myself go limp over the block, utterly defeated, wet with sweat, spunk dribbling from my nose and anus, punished and compliant, my only hope that they would make me come before they were done with me. Rathwell could fuck me, or use my bottom, or do it in my mouth, I didn't care, just as long as they brought me off.

'Throw a blanket over her,' Hannah instructed, 'so just her arse is showing. Now see here, Amber, while Rathwell's having his fun with you, Maggie and me, we're going to be having ours with your pretty little girlfriend. That's part of the deal, see?'

I nodded, trying to hide a grimace, but failing. She knew how to get to me and always had, gauging exactly how I'd feel when I knew that Kay was down on her knees licking their cunts, or sucking on their teats, of having her beautiful bottom spanked, and all the while with me tied naked over a whipping block while Rathwell used me to fuck in, because that was how it was going to be, my anus or vagina a convenient hole for his cock, nothing more. The fact it was me his cock was in meant nothing to him, nothing at all, but for me it was the exact opposite, as they knew full well.

'Here we are then,' Leary said from behind me and a thick, rough blanket smelling strongly of goat had been thrown over my body, leaving just my bottom exposed.

'We're taking Kay into the caravan,' I heard Hannah say. 'When he's done, beat her.'

'Here's Rathwell,' Maggie said from further off. 'Now how's that then, a nice fat tart to fuck in?'

She laughed. I heard the squelch of a boot in mud, the bang of the caravan door, then nothing. Leary and Rathwell were behind me, I knew, and that they were deliberately playing games with my head, but that didn't stop my rising sense of panic as I waited under what was obviously the goat's sleeping blanket, in choking heat and near darkness, the musky smell of the animal thick in my nostrils. Still there was nothing, and I began to jerk in my bonds, and to beg, to be spoken too, to be touched, and to be fucked. Finally Leary responded.

'Jesus girl, but you're an eager one. He can't fuck you until his cock's hard, can he now?'

With that I felt something warm and firm press between my bottom cheeks, then a tongue as he began to lap at my cunt, long, even strokes, every one of which brushed on my clitty. My mouth came wide in ecstasy and I was babbling for more on the instant.

'All the way … all the way … all the way, please … oh, you bastard!'

He'd stopped, but he'd tasted my cunt and he knew what to do with me. I felt his weight on my back and I'd been mounted, his cock pushing between my cheeks, to rub in my slit, push again, find my well-buggered anus and fill the

202

slippery, gaping cavity of my rectum with hot, fat cock. I cried out in shock as my buggering began, then in ecstasy as his balls began to slap on my fanny, only for his erection to slip free after just a few strokes.

'Just do it!' I yelled. 'Fuck me, you bastard, up my bum or up my cunt, but fuck me!'

Again he'd begun to rut in my slit, and I stuck up my bottom in a desperate effort to let him in up my hole. It worked, my body once more bloating with cock, only not up my bottom, but in my fanny. I was soaking, both with my own juice and Leary's spunk, and he went up easily, all the way. This time my cry was of pure ecstasy, and as his cock began to pump in my hole I knew he was going to get me there. If Leary's balls hadn't hit the spot, then Rathwell's did, the thick, wrinkled skin of his monstrous scrotum rubbing directly on my clit as he fucked me.

It was also my first fanny fuck since James had taken me, and my first dirty one in ages, and made all the better by the awful circumstances of my surrender, tied naked and bum fucked first, a smelly old goat blanket thrown over my body, my girlfriend licking cunt in a caravan just yards away, all as I was humped by Rathwell. I screamed for the utter degradation of what was being done to me, and again as he picked up his pace and his huge, heavy balls began to thump harder on my cunt, then a third time as it all came together in not just one orgasm but one after another, so hard and so strong that as the final wave of pleasure broke over me my vision had gone red, then black as I passed out.

All I got for sympathy was another bucket of water over my head, followed by Leary's belt across my bottom as he began the beating Hannah had ordered. I barely felt it, too far gone to react even as the thick leather belt he was using cracked down across my bottom cheeks. He touched me up too, his thick, rough-skinned fingers splashing in my juice and the mingled spunk running from my well fucked cunt and anus, but the only effect was another, small, orgasm, like the aftershock of an earthquake, and with that he gave up.

'You're a hard one to punish, to be sure,' he said, gave me a final crack across my rump with his belt and turned to the caravan. 'She's done, Hannah, fucked and beaten, like you said, and he went up her arse and all.'

It was Maggie who appeared at the caravan door, then Hannah and last of all Kay, who was naked from the waist down and sporting a pink bottom. I managed a smile for her, which she returned as they reached me, Hannah looking down on my body at first critically, then in satisfaction.

'That'll do,' she growled, 'Same time next month then?'

I managed a weak nod.

'Same time next month.'